Be careful what you wish for. . . .

Elizabeth stood numbly in the center of the mall, watching the glittering Christmas display wobble and bob through eyes brimming with tears. She had never felt so tired. Frantic last-minute shoppers rushed around her, but she was too weary to get out of their way. She felt like a rock in a fast-moving river.

She stared at the line of fidgeting children who waited for their turn to tell Santa their wishes.

I know what I wish, Elizabeth thought as a tear trailed down her cheek. I wish I'd never been born.

She closed her eyes, swallowing a sob as more tears came, steady as the rain outside.

Bantam Skylark Books in the SWEET VALLEY TWINS AND FRIENDS series.
Ask your bookseller for the books you have missed.

SWEET VALLEY TWINS
AND FRIENDS

A Christmas Without Elizabeth

Written by
Jamie Suzanne

Created by
FRANCINE PASCAL

A BANTAM SKYLARK BOOK®
NEW YORK · TORONTO · LONDON · SYDNEY · AUCKLAND

To Taryn Adler

RL 4, 008-012

A CHRISTMAS WITHOUT ELIZABETH
A Bantam Skylark Book / December 1993

*Sweet Valley High® and Sweet Valley Twins and Friends® are
registered trademarks of Francine Pascal*

Conceived by Francine Pascal

*Produced by Daniel Weiss Associates, Inc.
33 West 17th Street
New York, NY 10011*

Cover art by James Mathewuse

*Skylark Books is a registered trademark of Bantam Books, a division of
Bantam Doubleday Dell Publishing Group, Inc.
Registered in U.S. Patent and Trademark Office and elsewhere.*

ISBN: 0-553-15947-X

Published simultaneously in the United States and Canada

*Bantam Books are published by Bantam Books, a division of Bantam
Doubleday Dell Publishing Group, Inc. Its trademark, consisting of the
words "Bantam Books" and the portrayal of a rooster, is Registered in
U.S. Patent and Trademark Office and in other countries. Marca
Registrada. Bantam Books, 1540 Broadway, New York, New York 10036.*

PRINTED IN THE UNITED STATES OF AMERICA

OPM   0 9 8 7 6 5 4 3 2

One

"Jessica Wakefield, I want you and your friends out of my bedroom *now!*"

Jessica stared at her twin sister in shock. Her friends stopped talking and stared, too. It wasn't every day they got to see Elizabeth Wakefield in a bad mood.

"Lizzie, Lizzie, Lizzie!" Jessica said, scolding her sister from the comfort of Elizabeth's neatly made bed. "Where's your Christmas spirit? We're having our first official Christmas party–planning meeting. You should be ashamed."

"Yeah," Lila Fowler agreed, running Elizabeth's comb through her hair.

Elizabeth dropped her backpack and made her way toward the closet, picking her way over several pairs of legs.

"Ouch, Elizabeth," Ellen Riteman complained loudly. "You just crushed my foot. And by the way, you weigh a ton."

"Why don't you move this meeting to *Jessica's* bedroom?" Elizabeth suggested. "I promise not to follow you in there or step on anyone."

"My room's a mess," Jessica explained.

Elizabeth rolled her eyes. "So maybe you should try cleaning it every decade or so."

"Why are you in such a bad mood?" Jessica asked. "You could at least try to be happy for me. I *did* get picked to be the new chairperson of the party committee, you know." She couldn't help grinning. "You haven't even congratulated me yet."

The Sweet Valley Middle School, where Elizabeth and Jessica were both in the sixth grade, was planning a huge Christmas party for the students and their families. Earlier that day Mr. Clark, the principal, had announced the students who would be in charge of organizing it.

"Fine. Congratulations," Elizabeth said. "Now will you go away?"

"Don't you realize what a major honor this is?" Jessica asked.

Lila yawned loudly. "It's not that big a deal, Jessica."

"Sure it is," Jessica argued. "I was chosen from

hundreds of applicants for my excellent party skills and all-around hostessing talents."

"You were chosen because the principal pulled your name out of a hat," Kimberly Haver reminded her.

"That's what he told *you*," Jessica said, tilting her chin. "But that was just to ease the pain of your rejection."

"So this is your committee?" Elizabeth asked.

"This is it. Although they're really just my advisers," Jessica explained. "I have the final say on the party theme. I am all-powerful."

"Funny," Elizabeth said dryly, "your committee meeting looks just like a Unicorn meeting."

"Of course it does," Jessica said. "Nobody knows more about parties than the Unicorns."

The Unicorn Club was an exclusive group of the prettiest and most popular girls at Sweet Valley Middle School. To remind everyone of their special status, they wore purple, the color of royalty, every day. Not that anyone really needed to be reminded. Everyone knew the Unicorns were the most important girls in school—well, almost everyone. Elizabeth, who had actually refused to become a member, called the Unicorns "The Snob Squad." Jessica loved her twin, but sometimes Elizabeth didn't take important things—like the Unicorn Club—seriously. Of course, she took lots of other things seriously—her schoolwork, her job as the editor in chief of *The Sweet Valley Sixers*, the sixth-grade newspaper, or lately the volunteer work she'd been doing at the homeless shelter.

Sometimes it was tough believing they were actually identical twins. Sure, they looked alike, right down to the tiny dimples in their left cheeks. And they shared the same long, sun-streaked golden hair and blue-green eyes the color of the ocean. But when it came to things like boys and clothes and parties, Elizabeth and Jessica were very different people.

"You know, Elizabeth," Jessica said, "I'm not sure you understand how important this party is."

"Sure I do," Elizabeth replied. "Mr. Clark did appoint me treasurer, you know. I'm the one holding on to the money everybody raised."

"Yeah, but that's only because you're so trustworthy," Lila pointed out. "It's not like anyone is asking you to do the hard work. All you have to do is count the money."

Ellen frowned. "How much do we have, anyway?"

Elizabeth shot Ellen a look of exasperation. Ellen had already asked that question at least twenty times. "We have exactly three hundred and eighty-six dollars."

"Wow. Three hundred and eighty-six dollars," Tamara Chase said. "That's a lot of money, isn't it? I mean, it's kind of hard to believe."

"Not when I think of all the brownies I baked for those bake sales," Lila moaned.

"Lila, everyone knows you didn't really bake those brownies," Jessica said. "You got Mrs. Pervis to bake them for you." Lila was one of the richest girls in Sweet Valley. She lived with her father and their housekeeper, Mrs. Pervis, in a mansion, and Lila had more clothes than the rest of the Unicorns combined. As far as Jessica was concerned, Mr. Fowler spoiled Lila rotten.

"Look," Elizabeth said grouchily, "I hate to intrude on the privacy of a Unicorn meeting, what with me being just a lowly, average, non-Unicorn. So—" she pointed to her door, "would you mind? I've got a ton of homework to do."

"OK, OK," Jessica said reluctantly. "Come on, guys."

"Do we have to?" Ellen griped. "Last time I was in your room, I found a moldy banana peel under your chair."

"I don't think so, Ellen," Jessica said firmly. "It was under my dresser."

"Out!" Elizabeth commanded.

"All right already," Jessica said as the rest of the Unicorns began to leave. "Just let me run one idea by you. How do you feel about a mistletoe dance?"

Elizabeth didn't answer.

"OK, I'll take that as a no. How about a come-as-a-Christmas-ornament party?"

"I'm warning you, Jess. I'm not in the mood."

"OK, I can take a hint, Scrooge," Jessica snapped. When the rest of the Unicorns were gone, she paused at the door. "Is anything wrong, Lizzie?"

Elizabeth stared at her reflection in her dresser mirror. "Not really," she said. "Except that I have a zit the size of Mount Everest on my chin. And I got a B-minus on my English test today."

"I don't believe it!" Jessica cried.

"Believe it," Elizabeth said. She pointed to her chin. "How can you miss it?"

"Oh, of course I noticed *that*," Jessica said. "I'm not blind. What I can't believe is that you got a B-minus on something. Not that there's anything wrong with a B-minus. I'd be thrilled with one. But you . . ."

Elizabeth sighed. "I guess I've just been working so hard lately at the shelter that I fell behind on my reading. I'm sorry if I'm being grouchy, but I actually *do* have a lot of homework to catch up on."

"Cheer up, Elizabeth!" Jessica said brightly,

giving her sister a pat on the back. "Vacation's just around the corner, and I'm going to plan the best Christmas party Sweet Valley Middle School's ever seen. That should get you in the holiday spirit. You can't be bummed out at Christmas. Even with a zit the size of a Christmas tree."

"You're right, Jess." Elizabeth smiled. "Maybe I'll go over to the shelter for a while. That always makes me feel better."

Jessica frowned. "Whatever works. Although, personally, a pint of double-fudge chocolate-chip ice cream always does the trick for me."

Elizabeth laughed, but Jessica could tell she was still down in the dumps. She wanted to help, but she couldn't think of anything more to say. Then it hit her.

"Cover Magic!" she exclaimed.

"What?"

"For your zit. There's some in my medicine cabinet. It's like pimple camouflage." She grinned. "Trust me, Lizzie. It'll make a molehill out of your mountain."

On her way to the homeless shelter, Elizabeth passed a small drugstore. She caught sight of her reflection in the display window and groaned. Jessica had been wrong. Even with a big glob of

Cover Magic, her pimple wasn't disguised. *Oh, well*, she told herself. There were worse things than pimples.

She decided to go into the store and buy some red and green crepe paper to help decorate the shelter. It would mean spending some of her Christmas-present money, but she knew her family wouldn't mind if she scrimped a little this year on gifts. The families at the shelter had so little, it seemed like the least she could do.

The shelter was a long, low building painted pale yellow. It had a separate day-care center where children could stay while their parents went to job training or looked for work. The center was colorful and warm, full of donated toys and bright posters. But Elizabeth never went inside without feeling a twinge of sadness for the children who had to stay there. No matter how nice it was, it wasn't home, and it never could be.

As soon as Elizabeth opened the door to the center, a group of children came dashing toward her, shouting happily.

"Aren't you popular?" said Connie, one of the shelter workers. "What's in the bag?"

"Crepe paper," Elizabeth said. "I thought maybe we could decorate a little."

"Good idea. This place could use a little perking up."

"Lisbet!"

Elizabeth turned to see two of her very favorite shelter residents rushing toward her. Suzannah and Al—short for Alexandra—Glass were sisters. They'd been staying at the shelter ever since their parents had lost their jobs.

"Hey, Elizabeth," Suzannah said. She was eleven and had short brown hair and thoughtful green eyes.

"Lisbet!" shouted Al, who was four. Her long red braid flew behind her crazily as she ran. She grabbed hold of Elizabeth's leg and held on tight. "What did you bring me?"

"Let her go, you monkey," Suzannah said with a laugh.

"Here, Al," Elizabeth said. "Want to help me decorate?"

"You guys go ahead," Connie said. "I'll work on fixing the afternoon snack."

"What kind of snack?" Al demanded.

"Peanut butter and jelly."

"That's my favorite," Al said.

Connie laughed. "You say that every day."

"How was your day?" Suzannah asked Elizabeth as they began to twist the crepe paper from one corner of the room to the other, using tape to hold it in place.

"Pretty lousy," Elizabeth said. She started to

complain about her pimple and her disappointing grade, but then she remembered—no matter how hard her day had been, Suzannah's must have been worse. After all, Suzannah had been uprooted from her old school and the home she loved. Now she had to spend the day in a tiny classroom with kids from many different grades. A tutor hired by the county came to the shelter to give lessons.

"Actually, my day was fine," Elizabeth corrected herself.

"Mine was pretty great," Suzannah said enthusiastically. She taped her crepe paper to the wall and beckoned Elizabeth over. "Cross your fingers."

"OK," Elizabeth said, obeying.

"My mom got a part-time typing job yesterday," Suzannah said with a big grin.

"Suzannah, that's wonderful!" Elizabeth knew that Mrs. Glass had been out of work for the last three months. She'd had to take several weeks off from her secretarial job when Al got really sick with pneumonia, and she'd gotten fired.

"But that's not even the best part," Suzannah said. "She thinks she may have found us an apartment we can afford. Do you realize what that means? It means we might not have to spend Christmas at the shelter. We might be in our own home!"

"I'm so happy for you!" Elizabeth exclaimed.

"We're getting a house! We're getting a house!" Al sang, dancing in a circle with a crepe-paper tail streaming behind her like a snake.

"Not a house, an apartment," Suzannah corrected. "And it's not for sure, Al. Understand?"

"We're maybe getting an apartment, we're maybe getting an apartment!" Al sang, and soon several of her friends were joining in.

Elizabeth laughed. "This calls for a celebration," she said. "Extra jelly on our sandwiches, and glasses of milk all around!"

Suzannah sighed. "I know I shouldn't get my hopes up, but it's hard not to get excited, you know? And what the heck. It can't hurt to hope, can it?"

Elizabeth nodded. Suddenly all her silly problems, her B-minus and her pimple and her grouchy mood, seemed a million miles away.

"I'm hoping with you, Suzannah," she said.

"What do you think about a reindeer party?" Jessica asked at dinner that night. "You know, where everyone comes dressed as a reindeer? Rudolph, Prancer, Dancer . . . um, Blister, Goner, Cuba . . . you know. All those reindeer guys."

"I'd say it's a unique concept," Mrs. Wakefield said, trying not to laugh.

Jessica reached for a roll. "OK, forget the reindeer. How about Santa's elves?"

Steven, the twins' fourteen-year-old brother, laughed. "Great idea, Jess. You can go as Dopey."

"Those are dwarves, Steven, you dweeb," Jessica snapped. "We're talking elves."

"Dwarves, elves, munchkins." Steven shrugged. "No matter what you come up with, it's guaranteed to be the dumbest Christmas party in history."

Jessica threw a small piece of a roll at him, but Steven just caught it and popped it in his mouth.

"How about a sock hop?" Mr. Wakefield suggested. "Or maybe a sixties Christmas dance? Your mother and I could lend you our old records—"

"Dad, you are such an old fogey!" Jessica moaned. "Why would anyone want to listen to your ancient, fuzzy old records?"

"Ancient?" Mr. Wakefield cried. "Do you realize your mother and I once won an all-night dance marathon? *Twisting the Night Away*, it was called."

"Your father did an amazing twist," Mrs. Wakefield said. "Almost as good as Chubby Checker himself."

"Chubby Checker?" Steven said, looking mystified.

Mr. Wakefield shoved his chair back and began demonstrating, twisting back and forth and humming.

"Quick!" Jessica cried. "Someone do the Heimlich maneuver! Dad's choking on something."

"Very funny," Mr. Wakefield said good-naturedly. He sat down and put his arm around Mrs. Wakefield.

Elizabeth laughed, listening to her family tease one another. She gazed at the table filled with food, at the warm, inviting kitchen, at the cozy family room.

She thought of Al and Suzannah and crossed her fingers. If only they could have what she had. That would be the best Christmas present in the world.

Two

"All right, I'll ask you," Lila said the next day at the Unicorner, the table in the cafeteria where the Unicorns always ate lunch. "You've been waving that notebook around and scribbling notes in it every two seconds. Obviously you want one of us to ask you about it."

"Notebook?" Jessica said innocently. She held up the bright-red spiral notebook. "*This* notebook?"

"Do you see any other notebook?" Janet Howell asked.

"I just wanted to be sure you meant *this* notebook," Jessica said. "You see, this isn't just any notebook. This is the notebook that will help decide the fate of the Christmas party. This notebook is a symbol of my awesome power and responsibility."

Lila rolled her eyes. "Quick, somebody. Hand over the barf bag."

Mandy Miller laughed. "Don't you think you are kind of . . . uh . . . letting this go to your head a little, Jess?"

"I am not letting it go to my head. I'm just trying to be perfectly fair," Jessica protested. She opened the notebook and shoved it into Lila's face. "See? Already I have thirteen ideas. I'm listening to everybody. Even to total geeks."

"It's democracy in action," Janet said sarcastically as she opened her sandwich.

"Well, I think the Unicorns should get to decide," Ellen said.

Belinda Layton shook her head. "That wouldn't be fair, Ellen."

"Belinda's right," Jessica agreed. "*I* should decide."

"You just like lording it over everybody," Lila said with a sneer.

"It's my duty to give the little people a voice in the decision-making process," Jessica said importantly.

"Hey, Jessica, can I ask you something?" Ken Matthews called from the lunch line.

"Speaking of little people," Jessica said under her breath. Ken was one of the shortest guys in the sixth grade.

Jessica nodded to Ken, and he carried his lunch tray over. Winston Egbert was right behind him.

"We've got a killer idea for the Christmas party," Ken said.

"How nice," Jessica said, flashing an I-told-you-so look at Lila. She reached for her notebook and pulled a pen from her backpack.

"Well, actually it's Winston's idea," Ken admitted. "You tell them, Winston."

The tips of Winston's ears turned red. "Well," he began, "this is not your typical glamorous Unicorn kind of party idea, but how about a Christmas of the Future party? You know—all high-tech and computerized."

"Christmas of the Future," Jessica repeated without emotion. As part of her position, she'd made it a policy not to laugh at any idea, no matter how stupid. But Winston wasn't making it easy.

"I don't get it," Ellen said.

"That's because there's nothing to get," Tamara said. "A party has to have a gimmick, Winston."

"But this does!" Winston protested. "Santa could have a solar-powered sleigh. His gift lists would all be on computer. And the computer would determine the most efficient route for him to take from one house to the next, keeping track of which chimneys are wide and which are too narrow. Randy Mason and I are already working on the program."

"Don't forget the part about satellite hookups that would allow one Santa to appear in every mall simultaneously as a holograph!" Ken said enthusiastically.

"I don't get it," Ellen said.

"And instead of regular Christmas cookies, we could have them in tubes like the astronauts," Ken added.

"A very, um, unique concept," Jessica said. On her list she wrote *#14—Christmas of the Future— Winston and Ken.* Next to that she drew a small candy cane.

"What's the candy cane for?" Winston asked.

"That's my own private rating system," Jessica explained. "The more candy canes, the better the idea."

"How come we get only one candy cane?" Ken complained.

"Sorry." Jessica shrugged. "You lost a cane with that cookies-in-a-tube thing. But you can trust me to be completely fair and unbiased."

"Come on, Ken," Winston muttered. "Let's go eat. Our mystery meat's getting cold."

Jessica put down her notebook and opened a

bag of potato chips. "I'm always here, if you think of another idea," she called out cheerfully.

Lila grabbed Jessica's notebook. "Let me see this thing. Who has the most candy canes so far?" She scanned the list. "How come Janet got *four* candy canes?"

"Because my idea is brilliant," Janet replied. "I want the Boosters to dress up in new red-and-green cheerleading outfits and provide entertainment. The theme of the party will be *Catch the Holiday Spirit*."

"I don't get it," Ellen said.

"Think, Ellen. Why do the Boosters exist?" Janet said.

"To be the center of attention at pep rallies?"

"We're there to help increase school *spirit*. That's why my slogan's so perfect. Holiday spirit, school spirit. Get it?"

"It's great," Ellen said.

"Brilliant," Lila added.

"Well, it did get four candy canes," Janet said proudly.

Suddenly her eyes went wide. "Cute guy alert!" she said under her breath.

Jessica spun around to see Denny Jacobsen, one of the cutest guys in eighth grade, coming down the aisle. He had a soccer ball under his right arm.

"Hi, Denny!" Jessica called.

"Don't say hi to him!" Janet hissed. "I have *hi* priority."

Jessica turned back. "Since when?"

"Since she has the biggest crush on him," Ellen explained in a whisper. "You know how Janet gets around Denny, Jess. It's like she turns into a babbling ball of Jell-O—"

"Shut up, Ellen," Janet commanded, tossing a carrot stick at her. "It's since I saved his life, that's when." A while before, Janet had run into Denny and knocked him down right before he got knocked down by a huge, speeding papier-mâché tooth. He had seemed pretty grateful at the time.

"Hi!" Denny said as he sauntered up. "What's up? Food fight?"

"We were just teaching Ellen about the four basic food groups," Janet said. "What brings you to the Unicorner?" she asked sweetly.

"Actually, I'm here to see Jessica," Denny said.

Jessica cast Janet a smug grin.

"I have a great idea for a Christmas party," Denny said. He took his soccer ball and spun it on the tip of his index finger. "A big Christmas soccer game."

"Brilliant!" Jessica cried. "Why don't you sit down next to me, and I'll write down all the details." She reached for her notebook while Denny straddled the chair next to hers.

"Well," Denny began, "I was talking to the other guys on the team, and the way we see it, everybody loves soccer, right?"

"Absolutely," Jessica said.

"And who wants to go to some boring, prissy dance where everybody sits around eating little cookies, right?"

Jessica nodded. "Absolutely."

"So we figured, we'll provide the entertainment, and everybody will have a great time!" Denny continued.

"Maybe the Boosters could be there to cheer you on," Janet suggested.

"What?" Denny turned toward Janet. "Oh, yeah, sure, if you want. I guess it couldn't hurt."

"*Soccer game*," Jessica wrote in her notebook. Denny looked over her shoulder as she wrote. Up close, he was even cuter. Jessica wondered if he was really interested in Janet.

"What are those things?" Denny asked.

"Candy canes," Jessica explained.

"Why are you drawing ten of them?" Denny asked.

"*Ten?*" Janet exploded. "I got only four!"

Jessica smiled sweetly. "I told you, Janet. I'm completely fair and unbiased."

*   *   *

"You sure have been coming here a lot lately," Amy Sutton said to Elizabeth as they headed to the shelter that afternoon. "I feel guilty. I've been so busy with Boosters practice and holiday stuff, I haven't been here in a couple weeks."

"That's OK. They're always glad for the extra help," Elizabeth said. They paused at the back gate of the fence surrounding a small playground. Bright yellow swings rocked in the cool breeze. "Remember Suzannah and Al?"

"How could I forget them? Al nearly wore me out last time, begging me to push her on those swings."

"Well, I think they may be getting an apartment," Elizabeth said. "Don't say anything, though, just in case it falls through. Suzannah and Al really have their hopes up."

But as soon as they stepped inside, Suzannah ran to greet them. "You won't believe this," she said breathlessly. "My dad called today. He's been up north looking for work, because he just couldn't find anything around here. Anyway, he finally got a job doing some construction. And guess what?"

"I'll tell Lisbet!" Al cried. "Daddy's sending money so we can have a 'partment!"

"That's wonderful!" Elizabeth exclaimed.

"He thinks his boss will give him an advance on his pay," Suzannah explained. "That way my mom can put a deposit down on that apartment she was looking at."

"When will you know for sure?" Amy asked.

"He's going to talk to his boss tomorrow," Suzannah said. "And the manager of the apartment promised my mom he'd hold it until she found out for sure. Wasn't that nice? It's like suddenly everything is starting to work out."

"Let's go see the 'partment!" Al cried.

"Al," Suzannah said, "Mom already took us to see it once today."

"But Amy and Lisbet haven't seen it," Al said, tugging on her sister's hand. "Come on. Ple-e-e-eze?"

"Maybe we could a little later, Al," Elizabeth said gently. "We've got a ton of sandwiches to make first."

"Go on ahead," Connie called. "If I know Al, she won't stop talking about it otherwise."

"We won't be long," Elizabeth promised.

"Come *on*," Al said, rushing to the door.

"Sorry," Suzannah apologized as she, Amy, and Elizabeth stepped outside. "I know this must not seem like a big deal to you. But after all this time in the shelter, this apartment looks like heaven to us."

"Of course it's a big deal," Elizabeth said. "I think it would be so wonderful if you could move in before Christmas."

"Talk about a great Christmas present," Amy agreed.

"Turn here!" Al called at the corner.

"Wait for us, Al!" Suzannah yelled.

Suzannah took Al's hand as they turned the corner onto a quiet, tree-lined street. "See our street?" Al asked. "We have birds and trees, and there's a firedog next door."

"A dalmatian," Suzannah corrected as she pointed to a small, red brick apartment building. Al ran up a walkway lined with low green bushes. She crossed the yard and headed for a bottom-floor window on the left side of the building.

"Here!" she called, jumping up and down as she tried to get a glimpse through the window. "Here's our 'partment!"

Suzannah lifted her up so she could see inside. Elizabeth and Amy peeked in, too. A sunny kitchen opened onto a small living room with hardwood floors and fresh white walls.

"It's small, I know," Suzannah said, almost sounding apologetic. "But to us it looks luxurious."

"It has a bafroom too," Al pointed out.

Suzannah laughed. "You know what I've missed most since we moved into the shelter? Quiet. It seems like there's always noise, day and night. I used to love to curl up with a good book in my bedroom and just get lost in it. But at the shelter there's never any real privacy, you know?"

Elizabeth thought of her own big bedroom, of her library of Amanda Howard mysteries, of all the luxuries she took for granted every day. "I know it's all going to work out OK, Suzannah," she said.

"Come on," Al said, leaping from her sister's arms. "You haven't seen the bestest part!"

She dashed around the corner. The older girls followed. There, in the backyard, behind a low, chain-link fence, was a little swing set.

"My very own swings," Al said proudly. "Just what I asked Santa for."

"Jessica, I've got the perfect idea for a Christmas party," Brooke Dennis announced in the crowded girls' bathroom before first period the next day.

Jessica stopped combing her hair and pulled her red notebook out of her backpack. "All right," she said with a long-suffering sigh. "Just let me get a pen."

"Looks like Jessica's getting tired of her power," Amy whispered to Elizabeth.

Elizabeth laughed. "Are you kidding? She's loving every minute of it."

"Yesterday afternoon she told me she was up to forty-two ideas," Maria Slater said, shaking her head.

"Now, if this involves coming as your favorite elf," Jessica told Brooke, "it's too late. Three other people have suggested that idea. Also, I don't want to hear anything more about reindeer."

"My idea's much better than those," Brooke said. "I'm thinking more of a Hollywood-style Christmas party. Come-as-your-favorite-celebrity, maybe."

"I love it!" Jessica exclaimed.

"Extra candy canes for you, Brooke," Amy teased.

Sophia Rizzo and Sarah Thomas made their way through the crowded bathroom. "Are you still taking ideas, Jessica?" Sophia asked. "Because we've got a great one!"

"She already likes my idea," Brooke said.

"That's funny," Janet said as she applied lip gloss. "I thought she liked *Denny's* idea."

"I like everyone's ideas," Jessica replied defensively. "I'm very . . . uh, likeable."

"Then how about this?" Sarah said excitedly.

"A Christmas luau!"

Jessica narrowed her eyes. "You mean . . . like they have in Hawaii?"

"This wouldn't have anything to do with the fact that your parents just got back from their honeymoon in Hawaii, would it?" Maria teased. Sarah's father and Sophia's mother had recently gotten married, which meant that Sarah and Sophia were now stepsisters.

"Well, they *did* bring us grass skirts that we're dying to wear," Sophia admitted with a laugh. "But don't you think a luau would be fun?"

"I don't know," Jessica said doubtfully. "When I think Christmas, I don't necessarily think roasted pig and hulas."

"Oh, but you *do* think soccer game?" Janet demanded.

"Soccer?" Brooke cried. "What does soccer have to do with Christmas?"

"Soccer has to do with Denny," Janet said.

Brooke peered over Jessica's shoulder at her notebook. "How many candy canes did the luau get, anyway?"

"Jessica!" Melissa McCormick called, hurrying into the bathroom. "I have a great idea for you."

"All right, all right. Everybody calm down and be quiet," Jessica ordered in an official-sounding voice. "Now, let's hear your ideas one at a time."

Elizabeth couldn't help smiling as she and Amy and Maria sailed out of the bathroom. "Jessica loves all this attention. I have a feeling she's going to milk this thing for all it's worth."

Amy laughed. "She's not going to make a decision until the day before the party."

"Or until somebody wrings her neck," Maria added.

"I'm glad I'm just the treasurer," Elizabeth said. "There's nothing complicated about that."

Three

"Did you know that no two snowflakes are exactly alike?" Elizabeth asked Al the next afternoon. They were sitting cross-legged on the floor at the day-care center, cutting out paper snowflakes for the shelter's Christmas tree.

"All of Al's look alike," Suzannah teased, pointing to the pile of crude cutouts on the floor.

Just then Elizabeth noticed Mrs. Glass in the doorway. She was a petite woman with dark hair pulled back in a ponytail. Usually she had a bright smile, but today her mouth was drawn in a tight line and her eyes were red and swollen.

"Girls?" she said softly as she approached. "We need to talk for a minute."

Elizabeth started to leave, but Mrs. Glass motioned for her to stay. "That's OK, Elizabeth," she said. "You'll hear soon enough."

"What's wrong, Mom?" Suzannah asked, her voice tense. "Did something happen to Dad?"

"No, no," Mrs. Glass soothed. "Nothing like that, thank goodness." She sat down on the floor and gathered Al into her lap. "He just called me on the phone at the shelter office. He talked to his boss about getting an advance on his pay."

"And?" Suzannah asked hopefully.

"And the answer's no. Money's tight, and his boss wanted to help, but he just couldn't swing three hundred and seventy-five dollars right away. So—" She shrugged. "I guess you know what that means."

"No 'partment?" Al asked, eyes wide.

Mrs. Glass kissed the top of Al's head. "Just not this apartment, honey. There will be others."

Tears pooled in Al's huge brown eyes. "But this one had a swing set!"

"I know, hon," Mrs. Glass said. "We're all disappointed. But look on the bright side. Mommy's got a new job, and pretty soon we'll be able to find another apartment. And in the meantime, you have all your nice friends here at the shelter. And at least we'll have a roof over our heads on Christmas. That's more than a lot of people can say."

"I'm really sorry, Mrs. Glass," Elizabeth said,

feeling a heaviness in her chest. She looked over at Suzannah. She was busy cutting out snowflakes, her face expressionless. "Maybe you could talk to the landlord and ask him to give you a little more time," Elizabeth suggested.

"He's already held it a couple extra days just to be nice." Mrs. Glass shook her head. "I can't ask him to wait any longer. There's a waiting list of other people who'd love to have it. And we'll find another apartment."

"But not *that* one," Al protested, her voice suddenly racked with sobs. "We were going to have our very own rooms so Suz could read books and I would hardly ever bother her."

Suzannah looked up. "You never bother me, monkey," she said quietly.

"Come on," Mrs. Glass said, getting to her feet. "Let's you and me go try out the swing set here, Al." She touched Suzannah gently on the shoulder, then turned and led Al toward the playground.

Elizabeth watched them go, feeling an ache of sadness in her throat. "I know how disappointed you must be, Suzannah," she said at last.

Suzannah threw back her shoulders. "That's all right," she said flatly. "I'm getting used to it."

Three hundred and eighty-six dollars. Elizabeth

sat in her closet that evening, the light on and the door closed, staring at the money in the little metal cash box. She thought of all the work people had done in the last month to make that much money— all the bake sales and car washes. Gingerly she reached into the box and lifted the wad of wrinkled bills as if they could burn her fingers.

The door flew open. Elizabeth gasped. She clutched the money to her chest, her heart pounding.

"I just heard idea number fifty-six," Jessica announced. She peered more closely. "What are you doing with our money?"

"I was, uh, just recounting it," Elizabeth stammered. Quickly she returned the money to the box and hid it in a corner behind some shoes.

"You sure you weren't planning on stealing it?" Jessica teased.

Elizabeth stood. She could feel her cheeks burning. "To tell you the truth," she said, heading back into her room, "being responsible for all that cash kind of makes me nervous. I wish you'd just decide on a party theme and go on and spend it."

"That's what all the Unicorns keep saying," Jessica said. She stretched out on Elizabeth's bed. "But I keep telling them I need to give everyone a fair hearing."

Elizabeth sat at her desk. "I think you're enjoying all the power," she remarked.

"What power?" Jessica sighed. "This is a terrible burden, Elizabeth. I've got to talk to people day and night. I've been on the phone for the past two hours."

"What a strain that must be."

"Go ahead. Be sarcastic. But Mary Wallace just called, and do you know what she wants to do? Have a cookie party, where everybody brings a dozen of their favorite cookies!" Jessica rolled her eyes. "I mean, I like Mary—everyone does—but a *cookie* party?"

"I think it's a cute idea."

"That's why you're the treasurer and I'm the party planner. Cookie parties are for old ladies like Mom, Elizabeth. Besides, like I told Mary, we'd have tons of cookies left over, and *then* what would we do?"

Elizabeth glanced at the closet, where the money sat hidden. "You could give them to the homeless shelter."

"That's exactly what Mary suggested!" Jessica groaned. "Those people don't even have *homes*, Elizabeth. What do they want with a bunch of leftover cookies?"

"Jessica, sometimes you can be amazingly self-centered," Elizabeth said in annoyance.

Jessica grinned. "You're just now noticing this?"

Elizabeth shook her head. "I'm just saying that some people have more important things to worry about than party themes."

Jessica sat up on her elbows. "Is this because I didn't like the idea you and Amy came up with? *Christmas Throughout Literature?* No offense, Lizzie, but I just don't think anyone will get it. Besides, I gave you an extra candy cane just because you're my sister."

Elizabeth sighed. "Thanks and all, but would you mind getting out of here? I've got a bunch of *Sixers* articles to edit and a ton of math homework, and to tell you the truth, I'm having a hard time getting very worked up about your party problems."

Jessica scowled. "Grinch."

Elizabeth watched her leave. When the door was closed, she went back to her closet. For a long time she stared at the little metal box. She thought of all the balloons and food and fun the money inside could buy.

Then she thought of Al on her swing set, laughing as she flew higher and higher into the air.

The swing was going higher, higher still, so high that

Elizabeth felt sure she could touch the clouds. Below her, she could see her house . . . or was it her house? The windows were dark, but somehow she knew it was empty inside. Where was her family? She pumped her legs until she swung in a wider arc, and then she saw them— Jessica, Steven, her mom and dad, huddled on a corner, each carrying a battered suitcase. They had nowhere to go, Elizabeth knew, no home to call their own, no roof over their heads except the dark clouds hanging low. She pumped harder and harder. She didn't want to see. But no matter how hard she swung, they were always there, waiting for the storm clouds to burst. . . .

Her pillow was wet. Elizabeth's eyes opened wide. Was it raining? No, she realized. She'd been crying. She'd had a bad dream, that was all. Her family had been homeless. But it was just a dream. Here she was in her warm bed, with the sun spilling through the curtains.

All through breakfast and on the way to school, Elizabeth's thoughts kept turning back to the Glasses. When she stepped into the school entrance, with its red and green crepe-paper streamers and the Santa Claus cutout on the principal's door, it made her feel even worse. How could so many people be so happy when others were so sad?

"Boy, did you ever get up on the wrong side of the bed," Jessica muttered as they made their way through the crowded hall. "But that's the way you've been all week. I'm starting to get used to it."

"Sorry," Elizabeth said. "I guess I had a bad dream last night."

"So did I," Jessica said. "I dreamed I was the hostess at a huge ball. There was a soccer game going on in the middle of the ballroom. One team was wearing hula skirts, and the other team was dressed as reindeer and carrying computers. It was horrible."

They passed Todd at his locker. "Elizabeth!" he called, waving her over. "How come you didn't call me back last night? I left a message with Jessica."

"She told me," Elizabeth admitted. "I'm really sorry. I should have called back. I was so tired, I fell asleep kind of early last night."

"Good luck," Jessica warned Todd. "She's in a very Scroogy mood."

Elizabeth watched her twin head off toward a group of Unicorns gathered by Janet's locker. "She's right, I guess," Elizabeth said.

"That's OK," Todd said. "Sometimes all this holiday stuff gets to me too. I went shopping at the mall last night to find a gift for my mom, and it took me forever to find the perfect thing."

"What did you get?"

Todd closed his locker. "A catcher's glove." He grinned. "Perfect for *me*. Maybe you can help me shop for my mom tomorrow. I need a girl's point of view."

"Sure," Elizabeth said.

"You could try to sound a *little* bit interested," Todd teased.

Elizabeth thought for a minute. "Todd, I need your advice."

"Shopping advice? Unless it's for Steven, I'm pretty worthless."

"No, something else." She lowered her voice. "Do you think it's OK if someone does something wrong, but for the right reason?"

Todd leaned against his locker. "That depends, I guess."

"On what?"

"On what the wrong thing is that you're planning on doing."

Elizabeth looked away. "Who said it was me we were talking about?"

"Well, it's a pretty safe bet you're not talking about Jessica." Todd smiled. "She never thinks twice when she does something wrong."

Elizabeth sighed. "Not that I'm planning on doing it, but this wrong thing would make a lot of people angry. But it would also make a few people really happy."

"Those aren't very good odds," Todd said as the final bell rang. "Listen, we can talk about this more later. Maybe tomorrow while you help me shop."

Elizabeth nodded. "Tomorrow," she said, but she knew that tomorrow might be too late.

Four

The hardest part, Elizabeth realized, was figuring out a way to carry the money. She couldn't just put it in her backpack. Jessica was always nosing around in there for gum.

She couldn't just put it in her jeans pockets either. It was a big fat wad of mostly one-dollar bills—bigger still after she'd added her own Christmas savings money to it. Instead of buying her family presents, she'd decided that she could just make them something. Maybe she'd give her mom breakfast in bed, and do the dishes for a week for Steven. She could even volunteer to clean Jessica's room. That would be a bigger present than anything she could buy.

At last, after some thought, Elizabeth decided on her blue windbreaker. It had two large pockets in the front, big enough for the thick pile of money. She divided the cash in half and flattened it as well as she could into the pockets.

When she got downstairs, Mrs. Wakefield was making coffee and Jessica was drowsily pouring cereal into a bowl.

"You're already up and dressed?" Mrs. Wakefield exclaimed. "You do realize this isn't a school day, don't you?"

"I thought I'd go over to the shelter this morning," Elizabeth said.

"Don't you want to go shopping with me at the mall?" Jessica said with a yawn. "It's the last Saturday before Christmas, Elizabeth. Don't you care about tradition at all?"

"I think it's wonderful Elizabeth is spending so much time down at the shelter," Mrs. Wakefield said.

Jessica slumped into a chair at the table. "I know, I know," she muttered. "She's a saint. And I'm just a superficial party girl." She took a spoonful of cereal. "Oh, well, it's a dirty job, but someone's got to do it."

Elizabeth grabbed a doughnut and headed for the door. "I think I'll get going—"

"Hold on a minute." Steven appeared in the doorway. He had on his ratty blue bathrobe. His tangled hair stood up at odd angles. "Elizabeth is definitely *not* a saint," he said. "Do you realize what she's walking out of here with, the little thief?"

Elizabeth froze. Her throat seemed to tie in a knot.

"What are you talking about, Steven?" Mrs. Wakefield asked.

"Go on," Steven chided. "Admit it, Elizabeth. Tell everyone what you took."

"I—I—" Elizabeth stammered, her hand glued to the doorknob. She was afraid to turn around. She didn't want to see the look in Jessica's eyes when she learned the truth.

"Look at her," Steven said accusingly. "Can't you tell?"

Slowly Elizabeth turned. She'd been caught. Somehow, some way, Steven had seen her steal the money.

Jessica stared at Elizabeth's windbreaker, her eyes narrowed. "Wait just a minute," she said. "How did you manage that?"

"I know it's hard to understand, Jess," Elizabeth began. "I just wanted—"

"You are definitely more . . . boobular than usual," Jessica cried.

Elizabeth sneaked a glance at her chest. The money!

"That's not what *I'm* talking about," Steven

groaned. "She's wearing my last pair of clean socks in the entire universe! They were in a pile in the upstairs hallway with a bunch of clothes. I saw you swipe them, Elizabeth. 'Fess up or die."

Elizabeth felt her frozen limbs begin to melt. "I admit it," she said, nearly giddy with relief. "I am a sock thief. I didn't have any clean ones of my own."

"Told you she wasn't a saint," Steven muttered as Elizabeth opened the door to leave.

"And by the way, Lizzie—" Jessica called.

"Yes?"

"You're not fooling anyone with that Kleenex-in-the-pockets trick either!"

When she got to the shelter, Elizabeth peeked inside the day-care center first. *Good*, she thought with relief. Suzannah and Al were both there. That meant Elizabeth could talk to Mrs. Glass alone.

A worker at the shelter directed her to a small room near the end of a long hall. The door was open. Inside were six small beds and two battered dressers. Mrs. Glass was making her bed. Another older woman still slept, snoring softly.

"Mrs. Glass?" Elizabeth whispered.

She turned around, clearly surprised. "Elizabeth!" she said. She gave a wry smile. "What brings you to my humble home?"

"I was hoping we could talk for a minute."

Mrs. Glass led her out into the hall. "It's a little more private out here," she said. "Now, what's bothering you? Let me guess." She put her hands on her hips. "Al's been driving you crazy, is that it? She's grown so attached to you, you must feel like you have an extra arm."

Elizabeth smiled. Suddenly she felt very uncertain. What if Mrs. Glass refused to take the money? How could Elizabeth explain where it came from? She should have planned all this out on the way over. Usually she was great at that kind of thing. How many times had she helped Jessica reason her way out of a tough bind?

But this was different. This time it was Elizabeth who was in the bind.

"Tell me, honey," Mrs. Glass urged. "You look so worried. Whatever it is, I'm sure we can figure something out."

Elizabeth cleared her throat. "Did you tell the landlord you couldn't take that apartment yet?"

"I called him yesterday. He was so sweet too. Said he'd been looking forward to having Al around to get into mischief." She shrugged good-naturedly. "But hey—it's not the only apartment in the world, right?"

"I was thinking," Elizabeth began carefully.

How would Jessica handle this? she wondered. "Suppose you could get a loan. You know— enough money so you could put a deposit on the apartment just until you and Mr. Glass get paid?"

"A loan?" Mrs. Glass laughed dryly. "Honey, that's about as likely as me sprouting wings and flying on out of here. No bank's going to lend money to someone in a homeless shelter." She shrugged philosophically. "Not unless they have a few screws loose."

"How about the Bank of Wakefield?" Elizabeth said. She unzipped her pockets and removed the two wads of bills.

Mrs. Glass gasped. "What on earth are you doing, carrying around money like that?" she cried.

"I want you to have it."

"Not in this lifetime," Mrs. Glass said firmly. "Now put that away, quick."

"Just as a loan," Elizabeth insisted.

Mrs. Glass's face hardened. "Elizabeth," she said in a low whisper, "where exactly did you get that money?"

Elizabeth winced. She'd known this was coming. "From my savings account," she said.

Had her voice just squeaked? She felt a little dizzy. Was this how Jessica felt when she told lies?

Mrs. Glass took the money out of Elizabeth's hands. Carefully she rolled it into a tight ball and placed it back in Elizabeth's pocket. "You may be just about the sweetest kid in the world," she said with feeling. "And I can't thank you enough for thinking of us. But you know I can't take your money."

"Please," Elizabeth pleaded. "You have to. It's just a loan, Mrs. Glass. You can pay me back soon. You said yourself you'd be getting a paycheck early next week. You could give me most of it back before anyone—before I even knew it was gone." Her voice faded. "You have to. It's Christmas. I don't want you and the girls to be stuck living here for the holidays."

"There will be other holidays," Mrs. Glass said firmly.

Elizabeth felt her shoulders slump. This wasn't working out at all the way she'd hoped. She wished Jessica were here. Jessica was an expert at getting people to do what she wanted.

"I understand," Elizabeth said. "But the money wasn't really for you, Mrs. Glass. It was more for Suzannah and Al. Suzannah was really looking forward to having her very own room." Elizabeth started to walk away. "And Al," she added quietly. "Al really had her heart set on that swing set in the backyard."

She glanced back. Mrs. Glass's eyes were misty. "You're good, Elizabeth Wakefield," she said. "You're very good. But I just can't."

"It *is* a perfect apartment."

Mrs. Glass thought some more. "The thing is, Carl's going to try to come home for Christmas. He thinks he can hitch a ride with a friend of his who has a big eighteen-wheeler truck. He's getting paid Monday, so that would mean I could pay the whole thing back on Tuesday just as soon as Carl gets here. Still—" she frowned. "I'd feel better waiting. We can find another apartment. And what if something went wrong and I couldn't pay you back right away?"

"Nothing will go wrong," Elizabeth assured her. She took the money and pressed it into Mrs. Glass's palm. "Please take it."

Mrs. Glass stared at the money, and then at Elizabeth for what felt like a very long time. "There's a pay phone down the hall," she said at last. "Let's go see if that swing set's still available."

"Where have you *been*?" Jessica demanded as soon as Elizabeth stepped into the family room. Lila and Janet were sitting with her on the couch; the rest of the Unicorns were gathered in front of the TV, watching cartoons.

Elizabeth glanced around the room nervously. "I was at the shelter," she said as she took off her windbreaker.

"Well, we've all been waiting for you, Elizabeth," Lila said irritably. "We're going shopping for party decorations and we need our money."

"I looked in your closet, but the cash box was empty," Jessica said. "What did you do with the money, anyway?"

Elizabeth's stomach lurched.

"I bet she spent it all," Tamara teased. "Probably on books or something."

"How can you shop for party decorations?" Elizabeth asked. "You don't even know what the theme of the party is yet."

Janet crossed her arms over her chest. "That's exactly what *I* said."

"We're just going to buy some of the basics," Jessica explained. "Crepe paper, balloons, that kind of thing. Face it, whatever theme we pick, red and green are pretty safe colors for a Christmas party."

"If we decided on my holiday-spirit theme," Janet said, pouting, "we could go ahead and buy new Boosters outfits today."

"I'm sorry, Janet," Jessica said firmly, "but I told you. I have a lot of factors to consider."

"Like who you want to flirt with more," Janet grumbled. "Bruce or Denny."

"Could you two hold it down?" Ellen called from her position in front of the TV. "We're trying to concentrate."

"On a cartoon?"

"It's a very complicated plot, Lila," Kimberly explained. "See, Wile E. Coyote just bought a rocket backpack—"

"I'm dying of thirst," Elizabeth said, taking a few steps toward the kitchen. "Anyone want a drink?"

"First get our money," Jessica instructed. "Then die of thirst."

"Could you all please be quiet?" Tamara cried.

"Trust me," Lila said. "The Roadrunner will get away in the end. He always gets away, and the coyote always gets squashed or blown up. That's the whole point."

"Great. Now you've ruined it for us," Ellen complained.

The ringing phone interrupted their bickering. "I'll get it in the kitchen," Elizabeth volunteered, but Jessica already had her hand on the extension.

"I got it," she said. "Hello?"

Elizabeth began moving stealthily toward the kitchen, hoping for a temporary getaway, but Jessica waved to her. "Elizabeth, it's for you."

Elizabeth gulped. She stepped over assorted Unicorns and took the phone from Jessica.

"Hello?"

"Elizabeth?" a woman's voice said. "It's Mrs. Glass."

"Hi," Elizabeth said, trying to sound casual. "What's up? Is this about the day-care center?"

"What? Oh, no," Mrs. Glass said. "I just wanted to tell you what happened. I finally got hold of the landlord at the apartment and told him I had enough to put a deposit on the apartment. And would you believe our luck? He hadn't rented it yet!"

"That's good news," Elizabeth said evenly.

"It's great news. The girls are just ecstatic. And the best part is, he's going to let us move in tomorrow, even though we won't have the rest of the rent money until Carl gets here. It will be close, but it should all work out. We'll have enough to pay the rest of the rent *and* pay you back for your loan."

"How nice."

"I just wanted to thank you again, hon. And I promise we'll have that money back to you before you know it."

Elizabeth gazed at the Unicorns. *The sooner, the better.* "That will be fine," she said. "Maybe I'll see you tomorrow."

"Thanks again, Elizabeth. You're a real life-saver."

Mrs. Glass hung up and the line began to hum, but Elizabeth kept the phone glued to her ear. Every so often, she nodded or murmured as if she were still talking to someone. What could she tell the Unicorns? *Sorry, guys. I gave the party money to a stranger?*

Jessica looked over at Elizabeth. "Could you quit blabbing?" she demanded crossly.

"I'll be off in a minute," Elizabeth whispered, putting her hand over the mouthpiece.

"Who is that, anyway?" Jessica asked.

Elizabeth hesitated. "Someone from the shelter." She pretended to be concentrating on the conversation. "Uh-huh," she murmured. "I understand."

"That does it," Lila said, jumping off the couch. "Elizabeth will never get off the phone, and this cartoon's never going to end. By the time we get there, the mall will be closed. I say, let's go."

"What'll we do for money?" Jessica asked.

"*I'll* pay," Lila announced. "Daddy just gave me my allowance. And besides, it's not like we can buy much of anything until you decide the party theme. You can pay me back when Elizabeth gives you the money."

"That's wonderful!" Elizabeth exclaimed into the phone. *Thank you, Lila,* she thought with silent gratitude.

"Come on, gang," Janet said as she stood and stretched. "Lila's buying."

"Don't go spending all that money, Elizabeth," Lila called as she headed out the front door. "I expect to be reimbursed!"

With a huge sigh of relief, Elizabeth watched the Unicorns leave. She couldn't remember when she'd ever liked Lila quite so much.

Five

"How much is that Christmas tree?" Elizabeth asked. It was Sunday afternoon, and the elementary-school parking lot was filled with families searching for just the right tree.

"That one there?" the man in charge asked her. "That's a beautiful Scotch pine. It's thirty-eight dollars with tax."

Elizabeth gasped. "I didn't know trees cost so much."

She'd been hoping to find a tree for the Glasses' new apartment, but the only money she had now was the six dollars she'd managed to borrow from Steven that morning.

The man stroked his bushy white mustache. "How much have you got to spend?"

"Six dollars. Plus I have an emergency quarter

in my sneaker, in case I ever need to make a phone call."

"Hmmm. Six bucks and an emergency quarter. That's not even going to buy you a branch, young lady." He looked at her skeptically. "This tree for you?"

"For some friends of mine. They just moved out of the homeless shelter, and I wanted their new place to seem more . . . you know, Christmasy."

"You carrying this tree yourself, or do you have back-up?"

"Just me."

"How far you going?"

"Two blocks."

The man jerked his thumb. "Follow me. I know just the tree."

Elizabeth followed him past sweet-smelling trees of all kinds—long needled, short needled, towering, and squat. At the end of the row, he stopped and bent down. For a moment Elizabeth couldn't see anything. Then he turned around. In his hands was a beautiful little pine tree, about two and a half feet high, planted in a plastic pot.

"Long after all these other trees are gone, this tree will still be living," the man said.

"It's perfect," Elizabeth said. She reached out

to touch the soft, dark-green needles. "But how much is it?"

He handed the pot to Elizabeth. "We're having a special today. It's free to a good home."

Elizabeth grinned. "Thank you!" she said. "It *will* have a good home. You can be sure of that."

"Merry Christmas," the man said, winking at Elizabeth.

"Merry Christmas to you too," Elizabeth answered. For the first time, she was starting to feel the Christmas spirit after all.

When Elizabeth got to the Glasses' apartment, they were already unpacking their suitcases.

"Lisbet!" Al cried. "You brought us a Christmas tree!"

"It's beautiful!" Mrs. Glass exclaimed, giving Elizabeth a hug. "Just what we needed to make this place perfect." She shook a finger at her. "But haven't you done enough already?"

"The tree man didn't even charge me for it," Elizabeth said. "I promised him it would have a good home."

Mrs. Glass put the little tree in the living room. "Well, wasn't that sweet?"

"Come see my room, Elizabeth," Suzannah called from the hall.

Al tugged on Elizabeth's hand. "No, come see my swing!"

There was a knock at the kitchen door and Al ran to answer it.

"All settled?" an old man asked. He had intense blue eyes hidden behind thick glasses.

"Just about, Mr. Thorsan," Mrs. Glass called. "Come on in, please. Elizabeth, this is Mr. Thorsan, our landlord. Like I told you, he was nice enough to let us move in with only half the total money."

"Nice or foolish," Mr. Thorsan said. "But I did want to remind you, I'll need to see the rest of that money Tuesday at the very latest." He shook his head. "I'm a dang fool, letting you move in without the full amount, especially when I could have had plenty of other tenants, but this little lady—" He patted Al on the head. "—seemed to have her heart set on the place. What can I say? I'm an old softie."

"You are," Mrs. Glass said. "And I promise we won't let you down. Carl—that's my husband, the one who's working construction up north—will be here by Tuesday afternoon at the latest, and then I'll have the rest of the money. You'll see."

The old man pursed his lips. "I hope so." His voice took on a darker sound. "The last time I let someone in like this, they took advantage of me and I had to have them evicted. I wouldn't want that to happen to a nice family like yours. Not right before Christmas. But I've got to eat too, now, don't I?"

"Of course," said Mrs. Glass. "Don't worry, Mr. Thorsan. We're not going to take advantage of your kindness."

"Well." Mr. Thorsan turned to leave. "I'll be off, then."

Mrs. Glass closed the door behind him and frowned. "I hope we're not getting in over our heads."

"What do you mean, Mom?" Suzannah asked.

"Oh, nothing." Mrs. Glass waved her hand. "I'll just feel better when all the rent's paid up." She grinned. "Not that I don't feel pretty terrific already!"

"Come swing," Al demanded.

"I'll be there in a second, Al," Elizabeth promised. "First Suzannah's going to show me her new room."

Suzannah led her down a hall to a tiny room with pink rosebud wallpaper. There was a twin bed in a corner and a white chest of drawers nearby.

"Privacy at last," Suzannah said with a grateful sigh.

"It's great," Elizabeth said. "Just perfect."

"You know my favorite part?" Suzannah pointed to a little alcove with a built-in shelf where she'd lined up her books in a neat row. "I have a place to read in peace and quiet." She turned to Elizabeth. "My mom told me what you did, Elizabeth. How can I ever thank you?"

Elizabeth scanned the row of books and picked out one of them. "How about you lend me this book?" she said with a smile.

Forty-eight hours, Elizabeth told herself that afternoon on her way home from the Glasses'. Two more days until Mr. Glass got home and she could give Jessica the party money. She could lie for two more days, couldn't she? How hard could it be? Jessica did it all the time.

She'd been lucky yesterday. Jessica and the Unicorns had spent so much time at the mall arguing over the party theme that they'd ended up putting everything on hold. And Jessica had been on the phone all evening, debating party concepts.

Elizabeth turned the corner. Down the street she could see Steven in their driveway washing the van. Mr. Wakefield was putting Christmas lights on the mailbox, and Mrs. Wakefield was pruning one of the bushes. She had on her heavy work gloves and her blond hair was tied back with a bandanna.

Elizabeth felt a little surge of happiness as she walked along the sidewalk. She thought of the Glasses settling into their new apartment and making it a home of their own. She'd done the right thing, lending them the money. Suddenly she felt sure of it.

As Elizabeth headed up the front drive, Jessica came out the door. "Elizabeth!" she cried. "You're back. Good. I've been on the phone all afternoon. What do you think of a Christmas party with a jazz theme?"

"Whose idea was that?" Mrs. Wakefield asked.

"Patrick Morris. He loves to play the saxophone. I gave it eight candy canes."

Mr. Wakefield smiled. "Is that good or bad?"

"Pretty good."

"I didn't know you liked jazz, Jessica," Mrs. Wakefield said.

"I don't. But Patrick gets extra candy canes for being so cute."

"Isn't that sexist?" Steven asked.

Jessica pointed to the right fender of the van. "You missed a spot, Steven."

Steven smiled sweetly and turned the hose on Jessica.

"Steeeeeeven!" Jessica ran back into the house, screeching all the way.

Elizabeth followed Jessica upstairs into her room.

"That jerk!" Jessica exploded. She yanked open a bureau drawer and began digging for a dry pair of jeans. "He is such a juvenile delinquent! I wish Mom and Dad would send him to boarding school or something. I suggested it, but Mom acted like I was kidding."

Jessica gave up looking for a pair of jeans and sank onto her bed with a sigh of disgust. "I am *so* worn out. I never thought I'd say this, but I'm actually partied out. I'm sick and tired of talking to people about decorations and music and balloons." She sat up on her elbows. "Hey, I meant to ask you. Where *did* you hide that money, anyway?"

Elizabeth studied her nails. If she had to lie, at least she didn't want to look in Jessica's eyes when she did it. "I can't tell you, Jess," she said evasively. "How do I know you won't sneak off and buy yourself that purple cashmere sweater you've had your eye on for months?"

"Puh-leeze, Lizzie. You really think I'd do a thing like that? Moi? If I were going to steal that money, I'd at least invest in some jewelry."

Elizabeth laughed. "Trust me. I hid it in a very safe place."

"Under your mattress?"

"Give me some credit."

"In a sock?"

Elizabeth shook her head. "You're not even warm."

"I know! In the freezer! Ellen's mom does that."

"Too obvious," Elizabeth said. "My hiding place is much more original." *You can say that again,* she added silently.

Jessica groaned. "Tell me, Elizabeth, or I'll go crazy trying to guess. And it is my money in a way."

"No, it's everybody's money," Elizabeth replied, feeling a twinge of fresh guilt as she said the words. "And it's a lot of responsibility having that much cash." She headed for the door. "Besides, you've got enough on your mind, Jess."

"True. I never realized how tiring it is being powerful. No matter what I decide, tons of people are going to be mad at me. It isn't fair. The only reason I took this job was so everybody would—"

"Kiss up to you?"

"Well . . . yes."

Elizabeth paused. "When do you think you'll be needing the money, exactly?" she asked, trying very hard to sound casual.

Jessica sighed. "Don't *you* pressure me, too, Elizabeth!"

"I was only thinking—" Elizabeth cleared her throat. "Well, you know. The party's Christmas Eve. That's not much time."

Jessica pulled her pillow over her head and let out a scream. "Don't remind me!" she cried in a muffled voice. She tossed the pillow aside. "It's not my fault I'm indecisive. I'll decide when I decide. OK?"

"Fine with me," Elizabeth said sincerely. "Take all the time you need."

Six

"So what's it going to be, Jessica?" Denny asked as Jessica and Elizabeth walked into school Monday morning. He fell into step beside them. "If you're going with the whole soccer-game thing, I'll need to tell the team so we can get organized."

"Well, Denny," Jessica began, "that's a very good question. A *very* good question." She glanced over at Elizabeth, who was smirking. Jessica gave her a nudge in the ribs. "I've narrowed it down to just a couple ideas, and yours, I can definitely say, is a top contender. Right up there in the final few."

"Great." Denny grinned. He had a wonderful grin, Jessica decided. Wonderful eyes. Wonderful hair. It would be really wonderful if she could make him happy by deciding on his idea. Too bad it wasn't that simple.

"So," he continued, "when will you know for sure? Because we'd like to, you know, wash our uniforms and stuff."

"Very thoughtful," Elizabeth commented.

Jessica nudged her in the ribs again.

"Ow!"

"And isn't the party supposed to be the day after tomorrow?" Denny asked. "There's almost no time left."

"Like I said," Jessica replied uneasily, "I've narrowed it down to just a few contenders."

"Including yours truly," someone said.

Jessica spun around. It was Patrick. He also had a wonderful grin, come to think of it.

"What's *your* idea?" Denny asked.

"A jazz party. I figured we'd bring some music, and maybe some of my friends could jam a little."

Denny looked at Jessica. "I hope you buy plenty of earplugs with all that bake-sale money."

"No one said we're going to have a jazz party," Jessica pointed out.

"I thought you said you loved the idea," Patrick said, looking crestfallen.

"I *do* love the idea," Jessica said quickly. "It's definitely right up there in the final few."

"Who wants to hear you play your sax," Denny demanded, "when they can watch me and the guys kick goals?" He turned to Elizabeth. "What do you think, Elizabeth?"

"I think I'd better be going," Elizabeth said quickly. "Good-bye, Jess. Or should I say good luck?"

"So," Jessica said brightly, looking from Denny to Patrick and back again. "Back to the party question. How do you guys feel about luaus?"

When Elizabeth got to the *Sixers* office, she found Sophia and Amy going over stories for the next day's edition. "How's everything look?" Elizabeth asked.

Amy shrugged. "It's going to be a little short, but then again, it's the holiday edition. People will be too excited about vacation to pay much attention, anyway."

Sophia handed Elizabeth a piece of notebook paper covered with a messy scrawl. "We still have to type this up," she said.

"Let me guess," Elizabeth said. "It's Caroline Pearce's gossip column, isn't it?"

Sophia nodded. "She has the worst handwriting I have ever seen. I was going to start typing it up, but you're the only one who can decipher it, Elizabeth."

"I'll try to do it at lunch," Elizabeth said. "We're way behind on this issue, and I'm afraid it's my fault. I've been so busy with . . . well, stuff at the shelter. I let all this go till the last minute."

"Don't worry," Amy said confidently. "We'll get the paper out. Have we ever missed an issue yet?"

Elizabeth scanned Caroline's column. "I hope I can make some sense out of this."

Sophia pointed to the bottom of the page. "There's a section in there about Lila Fowler's newly redecorated room. I was going to edit it out, but since we need all the stories we can get, I guess we should leave it."

"Who could possibly care how Lila decorates her room?" Amy asked.

"No one but Lila," Elizabeth answered. "But Sophia's right. We may as well leave it."

"We could write up an article about the Christmas party," Amy suggested.

"We could if Jessica would only decide on a theme for it," Elizabeth said with a smile. "At the rate she's going, it may be New Year's before she comes up with one."

"After all those cars I washed," Sophia said. "I'll bet Jessica won't even have time to spend the money we raised."

"If I know Jessica, she could spend that much

money in about ten minutes," Amy said with a laugh.

"How much was it again?" Sophia asked.

"Three hundred and eighty-six dollars," Elizabeth said quietly.

Amy whistled. "That's a lot of cookie baking and car washing," she said. "But I guess it was all for a good cause."

"Did you ever think—" Elizabeth hesitated.

Amy peered at Elizabeth. "Think what, Elizabeth? You look so serious all of a sudden."

"I was just wondering if maybe we could have put all that money to better use somehow."

"What's better than a fun party for the whole school?" Sophia asked.

"I don't know," Elizabeth said. "A worthy charity or something."

"I like that idea," Amy said. "Maybe next year we could do that. But we'd have to get everyone to agree on it since we'd all chip in to raise the money."

Elizabeth stared at Caroline's column, but the words blurred together on the page. "You're right," she said quietly. "That would be only fair."

"Elizabeth?" Todd said, appearing at the door of the *Sixers* office after lunch. "Are you too busy to see me?"

Elizabeth looked up from Caroline's article. "Of course not," she said, surprised by his serious tone and the grim expression on his face.

"You sure?" Todd asked. "I mean, I can make an appointment—"

"Todd!" Elizabeth interrupted. "Is something wrong? You seem really mad."

"You'd be mad, too, if you'd been stood up."

"Stood up?"

Todd crossed his arms over his chest. "I thought we were supposed to go shopping together Saturday. I waited at the mall for almost two hours."

Elizabeth pounded her palm against her forehead. "Oh no! I completely forgot! I went over to the shelter Saturday to give Mrs. . . ." Her voice trailed off. "Never mind. It doesn't matter. I'm really, really sorry, Todd."

"I tried calling you all weekend. What did you do—take the phone off the hook?"

"Jessica's been talking nonstop to everyone in school about the Christmas party." She paused. "We *are* still going there together, aren't we?"

Todd stared at the floor, his mouth set in a line. "I told Ken and Winston I'd go with them instead."

"But I thought—"

"At least I can *count* on them," Todd said.

Without another word, he walked away.

Elizabeth sighed. She wanted to explain why she'd been at the shelter, and why she'd been so distracted lately. But that would mean telling him what she'd done with the money, and she didn't dare tell anyone about that. Not even Todd.

Mr. Glass will arrive tomorrow, she told herself. *And then everything will be fine.*

She crossed her fingers just to be on the safe side. Then she went back to work trying to decipher Caroline's handwriting.

"Elizabeth, I've been waiting here for hours for you to come home!" Jessica cried late that afternoon.

Elizabeth dropped her backpack on Jessica's floor and sank onto the carpet. "I've been typing *Sixers* stories since eighth period," she groaned. "My fingers are raw. I may never type again."

"You think you have problems?" Jessica held up a notepad. "I've narrowed the party themes down to seven. The Unicorns are breathing down my neck. They say if I don't decide right away, they'll come over here, take the money, and decide on a theme on their own."

Elizabeth looked up in alarm. "They wouldn't really do that, would they?"

Jessica looked worried. "They might. I wouldn't put it past them to try to overthrow me. Of course, first they'd have to find the money. I told them you'd hidden it and that even I didn't know where it was. They didn't believe me. Janet even threatened to torture it out of me. Something about fingernails."

"I know. Bamboo shoots under the nails."

"Worse." Jessica shook her head. "They were going to paint them a really putrid shade of orange." She scanned her list. "What am I going to do, Elizabeth? No matter what I decide, somebody's going to hate me."

"That's the price of power, I guess."

Jessica sighed. "Hey, by the way. That Suzannah girl called." She paused. "And then someone else called for you, too, I think. I've been on the phone so much, I've lost track. Anyway, Suzannah said she wanted to invite you over to her apartment tomorrow afternoon. Something about a welcome-home party for her dad?"

"Oh," Elizabeth said, trying not to sound too interested. "I'll call her back."

"I thought she lived in the homeless shelter."

Elizabeth cleared her throat. "She did, but they found a new place."

"That's nice," Jessica said. "I bet you helped them, right?"

"What do you mean?" Elizabeth asked nervously.

Jessica waved her hand. "Oh, you know how you are. Always helping people and being saintly and perfect so you can make me look bad." She grinned. "You know, it's not like this—" she waved her list, "isn't community service, too. We're talking a major good deed here. This party will bring families together. There'll be loads of holiday cheer. Goodwill toward men and all that stuff."

If there is a party, Elizabeth added to herself. She reached for her backpack and stood. "You know what I think you should do?" she suggested casually.

"Tell me, please!" Jessica begged.

"Sleep on it. That always works for me."

"But we need to go shopping," Jessica moaned. "It's Monday. The party's Wednesday evening."

"Give it another day." *Give me another day*, she added silently.

"I don't know. What if the Unicorns decide to mutiny?"

"You're the one in command," Elizabeth reminded her. "You can't let them push you around, can you?"

"No, I guess not," Jessica agreed doubtfully.

"Besides, the longer you wait, the greater the

suspense. Trust me on this," Elizabeth added, feeling guilty as she said the words.

"I do trust you," Jessica said. "I'll give it another day."

Elizabeth walked down the hall, Jessica's words ringing in her ears. She felt weighed down by guilt. When she'd decided to help the Glasses, she hadn't really thought about how much trouble she might be getting Jessica into.

She went into the bathroom and stared at her reflection. What kind of sister was she, anyway?

A conniving, lying, manipulative one, her reflection answered.

This was terrible. She was turning into Jessica.

Seven

Elizabeth had a very bad feeling when she woke up the next morning.

She'd been having a bad dream, a terrible dream. Something about money. She'd run out of paper for the *Sixers*, so she'd printed them up on dollar bills instead—the money that had been meant for the party.

She peered over her blanket. Pale, bleak light poured through the crack in her shade. She climbed out of bed and peeked out the window. It was raining. Not just raining. It was pouring. It was a monsoon. Huge drops slashed down from a dark gray sky. She and Jessica would need a raft to get to school.

Elizabeth trudged to the bathroom. She flicked on the light and stared at the mirror. A new pimple stared back at her. Her face had disappeared. It had been taken hostage by a pimple the size of New Jersey.

Yes, she had a very bad feeling about today.

Elizabeth had a very bad feeling when she ran into Todd in the hallway before homeroom.

"Have you forgiven me yet?" she asked hopefully.

Todd headed for his locker as if it were the finish line in a one-man race. Elizabeth dashed after him. "Please don't be mad anymore, Todd," she said.

Todd fumbled with his lock. "I was all set to make up yesterday, Elizabeth. But I guess you were just too busy."

"Yesterday? What are you talking about?"

"I *called* you yesterday afternoon," Todd said. He opened his locker and got out his notebook. "But hey. Don't worry about it. I'm kind of getting used to being ignored."

Elizabeth groaned. "Jess *said* somebody called, but she couldn't remember who it was. I'm really sorry, Todd. She's been sort of distracted lately."

"She's not the only one." Todd slammed his locker shut. "I'm sorry," Elizabeth said sincerely. "I've had a lot on my mind the last couple days."

"Is something wrong? You seem a little weird."

"Not really," Elizabeth said evasively. *Unless you count the fact that I'm a thief.*

"Fine," Todd said. "Talk to me again when you're back to your old self." He started to leave, then hesitated. "By the way, did something happen to your chin?"

Elizabeth had a very bad feeling when she ran into Lila a few minutes later.

Lila stalked up to her, her face set in a scowl. She was clutching a copy of the *Sixers* in her hand.

"I'll sue you for this, Elizabeth Wakefield!" Lila screeched. Traffic in the hallway came to a standstill. Elizabeth could feel dozens of pairs of eyes boring into her.

"Lila," she began, "what's—"

"My father doesn't have just *one* lawyer," Lila continued. Her face was nearly as purple as her blouse. "He has seventeen! Do you hear me? *Seventeen* lawyers!"

"Lila," Elizabeth said in a soothing tone, "what are you talking about? Sue me for what?"

"Libel!" Lila cried. "No, I mean slander!" She threw her arms in the air. "*You* know what I mean! You're the A-plus English student! You're the editor in chief of this slimy rag you call a paper."

Elizabeth took Lila's arm and pulled her toward the lockers. To her relief, traffic began to flow again, although a few people continued to stare.

"If there was something in the paper you didn't like," Elizabeth said calmly, "maybe you should write a letter to the editor. We could publish it in the next issue after we get back from vacation."

"You won't be coming back from vacation," Lila said. "You'll be in jail by then."

"For what exactly?"

"Libel. Slander. No." Lila shook her head. "It must be libel. Which is the one where you write something awful about somebody and cause them to be publicly humiliated right before the holidays on the eve of a very important Christmas party and make them so upset they cry and their mascara runs?"

"Hmm. That would be libel, I think." Elizabeth reached for Lila's mangled copy of *The Sixers*. "But to tell you the truth, I still don't have a clue—"

"There!" Lila pointed to Caroline Pearce's gossip column. "How would you feel if someone printed that about *you*?"

"I proofread Caroline's column yesterday," Elizabeth said as she scanned it. "And I typed it up myself. There wasn't anything—" Suddenly she stopped.

Lila Fowler has completely redecorated her broom. Elizabeth winced. "Oh, Lila," she said, flushing. "I'm really sorry. I was in a big hurry, and I guess I must have typed an extra *b* in there."

"That's not all of it," Lila snapped. "Keep reading."

Elizabeth looked back at the paper. *The decorations include a lot of purple, naturally, and also her very own TV and VCR. Fortunately, Lila's wich enough to afford it.* Elizabeth winced again.

"*Witch?*" Lila nearly shouted.

"Actually, *witch* is spelled with a *t*, Lila," Elizabeth explained. "Obviously it's just another typo. I hit *w* instead of *r*."

"So I'm supposed to believe that careful, perfect Elizabeth Wakefield made two errors, and they just happened to be *broom* and *witch*? Likely story."

"Look, I know it looks bad, but . . ."

"Tell it to the judge," Lila said. She snatched the paper away and stuffed it into her purse. "I'm saving this for evidence. And I've arranged to have the remaining copies destroyed."

"What are you talking about?" Elizabeth cried.

Again the traffic in the hall slowed to a crawl. "Are you crazy? You don't mean you—"

"Not me, the rest of the Unicorns. My loyal friends. They tossed the rest of the *Sixers* into the Dumpster out back."

"How could you?" Elizabeth demanded.

"How could I? How could *you*?" Lila spun on her heel and strutted off. She'd gone only a few feet when she glanced back over her shoulder.

"Oh," she said, "speaking of witches. I have the name of an excellent plastic surgeon who could remove that thing on your chin if you're interested."

Elizabeth had a very bad feeling when Jessica took her aside after homeroom.

"Did you have to write that about Lila?" Jessica demanded as they walked down the hall. "I'm under enough pressure right now, Elizabeth. I mean, sometimes she is kind of a witch, but that crack about a *broom* was way out of line."

"It was a mistake," Elizabeth protested. "A typo. I told her that. And you had no right to dump all those *Sixers*, Jessica!"

"I had nothing to do with that," Jessica replied. "Besides, they got rid of only about half of them. Mr. Bowman caught Ellen by the Dumpster red-handed."

As they turned the corner, Jessica noticed Denny and waved. "Look, let's call a truce, OK?"

"Sorry. I'm not having a very good day."

Jessica sighed. "Me neither. The Unicorns want to go shopping right after school."

Elizabeth swallowed past a hard knot in her throat. *She wouldn't have the money by then.* She paused at the drinking fountain and took a long, very slow drink.

"The problem is, I still haven't decided whose party idea to go with. I'm still torn between Denny, Bruce, Patrick, and Janet."

"Janet?"

"She scares me more than all three of the boys put together."

Elizabeth looked away. *She had to think fast.* "Jess, you can't go shopping right after school."

"Why not?"

Good question. "Because," Elizabeth said slowly, "because this morning I asked Dad to put the money in the bank for safe-keeping. And the bank will be closed before he can take it out."

Jessica's eyes went wide. "Why would you do a thing like that?"

"I don't know," Elizabeth said. "I was nervous having all that cash around."

"You've had it for ages," Jessica argued. "How come all of a sudden you're nervous?"

Elizabeth hesitated. "There've been a lot of burglaries in the neighborhood."

"What burglaries? I haven't heard anything about any burglaries."

"Don't worry," Elizabeth said, trying to sound cheerful. "We'll get that money first thing tomorrow morning. Look on the bright side. That gives you extra time to decide which people you want mad at you."

Jessica moaned. "This party's going to be a total flop, and everyone's going to blame me because I'm indecisive."

No, Elizabeth thought ruefully, *they're going to blame me because I'm a thief.*

"Well," Jessica said after a moment, "I guess there's nothing I can do."

"That's the spirit."

"Unless maybe I call Dad at work and ask him to stop by the bank before it closes."

"Bad idea," Elizabeth said firmly. "Very bad idea. Dad's got that big case today."

"What case? I don't know anything about a case."

"You know," Elizabeth said. "The big one. The really big one." Inside, she was cringing. She had never told so many lies in her life.

"Oh. I guess I forgot." Jessica sighed. "At least do me a favor, OK? You tell Lila about the bank. She's already furious with you."

"Deal," Elizabeth said, breathing a sigh of re-lief.

"I've got to go talk to Patrick," Jessica said. "I'm thinking about playing jazz music during a soccer game. You know—sort of killing two birds with one stone." She started to leave, then hesi-tated.

"What?" Elizabeth said.

Jessica reached into her backpack and re-trieved a small white tube. "Here," she said, pressing it into Elizabeth's palm.

"It's extra-strength Cover Magic. It won't make that thing on your chin disappear, but at least it won't be so . . . you know, *obvious*."

Elizabeth watched her twin disappear into the crowd. She looked down at the tube in her hand.

She had a very bad feeling about this day, and it had only just begun.

Eight

❄

When the bell rang that afternoon, announcing the start of Christmas vacation, Elizabeth was the first one out the door. She didn't want to have to talk to Todd or Jessica or Lila or the Unicorns. She'd just have to tell more lies, and she was getting very, very tired of lying.

She ran through the rain all the way to the Glasses' apartment, and the closer she got, the faster she ran. The sky was dark and the rain was cold and hard, but she didn't care. Soon she'd have the party money back. Soon she could stop lying to her sister and her friends. They could have their party. The Glasses could have their apartment. And Elizabeth could breathe a great, big sigh of relief.

"Elizabeth! You're soaked!" Mrs. Glass exclaimed when she opened the door.

Elizabeth stepped inside the cheerful kitchen. Two puddles formed at her feet. Outside, thunder cracked, shaking the windows.

"Lisbet!" Al cried. She and Suzannah ran into the kitchen. Both girls had red ribbons in their hair.

"What smells so good?" Elizabeth asked as she set down her soggy backpack and took off her raincoat.

"Peanut-butter chocolate-chip cookies," Suzannah said. "My dad's favorite."

"Is he here yet?" Elizabeth asked hopefully.

"No," Mrs. Glass said. "We thought he'd be here by now, but with the rain and all, he probably got delayed."

"Come see the sign we made," Al said, tugging on Elizabeth's arm. She pulled her into the tiny living room. On the wall over the couch was a hand-lettered sign. WELCOME HOME! it said. Al had drawn flowers around the edges.

"It's perfect," Elizabeth said. "I'll bet you can't wait to see him, can you?"

Suzannah gazed out the window at the rain gushing into the gutters. "I can't wait for him to see us *here*," she said. "The last time we saw him was two months ago, right before he went north to look for work. We'd just moved into the shelter." Her voice grew soft. "That was the only time I've ever seen my dad cry."

Mrs. Glass carried in a small plate of cookies. "Fresh from the oven," she announced as she set the plate on the coffee table. "Now, just one each, OK, girls?" She smiled apologetically at Elizabeth. "We could afford only one batch," she said, "so we need to make them last."

"They look wonderful," Elizabeth said, thinking back to all the times she and Jessica had made cookies by the dozens without thinking twice.

"Why isn't Daddy here yet?" Al asked.

"He'll be here," Mrs. Glass said. "They said on the radio there was snow up north. It's probably slowing down the driving." She joined Suzannah at the window. For a few moments no one spoke. The rain drummed on the roof. In the kitchen, the radio droned softly.

"Well," Mrs. Glass said, breaking the silence, "I'm going to go clean up in there. You girls keep yourselves busy."

For the next two hours, Elizabeth, Suzannah, and Al sat in the living room, cutting out paper snowflakes for the Christmas tree Elizabeth had brought. The more time passed, the less they spoke. Elizabeth could see the worry in Suzannah's eyes, and she could hear it in Mrs. Glass's loud, cheerful humming. Only Al seemed confident that Mr. Glass would arrive any moment.

Elizabeth felt horrible. She knew her friends were worried about Mr. Glass's safety. She was worried, too—but she couldn't help feeling guilty. They wanted him there because they loved him. She wanted him there because she needed the money he was bringing.

When it grew close to dinnertime, Elizabeth went to the kitchen. Mrs. Glass was sitting at the table, staring at the clock on the stove.

"I guess I should be going," Elizabeth said. "The rain's slowing down, and I told Jess to tell my mom I'd be home by six."

Mrs. Glass managed a smile. "I wanted Carl to meet you," she said.

"He'll be home soon," Elizabeth assured her. "Maybe you could all come to the Christmas party at the school tomorrow evening." *If there is one,* she added to herself.

"That would be—" There was a loud pounding at the door.

"Daddy?" Al cried, rushing into the kitchen.

"It's me—Mr. Thorsan," came a gruff voice.

Mrs. Glass swallowed. "He's already been here once today," she whispered. "He'll be wanting the rest of the rent money."

She stood, smoothed her dress, and went to

the door. Suzannah joined Elizabeth and Al. Her face was expressionless.

"Mr. Thorsan," Mrs. Glass said, opening the door to a gust of wet wind. "You'll catch your death out there. Please, come in."

Mr. Thorsan tramped inside. He was wearing muddy red galoshes and a black slicker. He took a white handkerchief out of his pocket and wiped his steamed-up glasses. "You got the rent?"

"Carl seems to be running a little late," Mrs. Glass said. "The radio said they're having quite a lot of snow up north. Maybe his ride got slowed up—"

"Or maybe he's not coming," Mr. Thorsan snapped. He shook his head. "Typical of you kind of people. The man runs off, leaves a wife and kids behind to fend for themselves."

"My dad's not like that!" Suzannah cried. "He went up north to get work. He's coming back, you'll see."

"I should have known better than to rent to a family from the shelter." The old man sighed. "And me, out of the goodness of my overworked heart, letting you move in on only half the money. Harold Thorsan, when will you ever learn?"

"I'm sure he'll be here soon with the money," Mrs. Glass said calmly. "Just give us a few more hours."

"I know, Mrs. Glass." Mr. Thorsan shook his head as if he were filled with regret, but his voice had a nasty edge. "I've heard it all before."

"It's true," Elizabeth said, her voice unsteady. "I'll vouch for them. Mr. Glass should be here any minute."

Mr. Thorsan stared at the sheet of cookies cooling on top of the stove. "May I?" he asked. When no one answered, he took one anyway. "I'd like to help you, really I would," he said to Mrs. Glass. "Here it is, nearly Christmas. And raining to boot. But charity goes only so far. You've gone and taken advantage of my goodwill." He bit into the cookie, chewing slowly. "What choice do I have but to ask you to leave?"

"Leave?" Al whispered.

"By tomorrow morning, I want you out," Mr. Thorsan said.

"But my husband . . ." Mrs. Glass said. "He may be here by then. And then you'll have the rent and we won't have to leave."

"Ten A.M., no later."

Mrs. Glass looked at Elizabeth. "If we do have to leave," she said, "what about my deposit?"

"It's already in the bank. I'll mail you a check."

"Where?" Suzannah asked. "Where will we go?"

Mr. Thorsan stuffed the rest of the cookie into his mouth. "Back to where you came from, I suspect."

"The shelter," Al whispered. Her lower lip was trembling.

"That's right, young lady," said Mr. Thorsan. "Don't blame me. I'm not your father."

He stepped back out into the rain, slamming the door behind him.

It's all my fault.

All the way home, Elizabeth kept telling herself the same thing. If only she hadn't tried to help. If only she'd minded her own business. It would have been better for Suzannah and Al if they'd never moved into the apartment, wouldn't it? Now it would be that much harder to go back to the shelter. . . . What if there wasn't even any room for them there anymore?

She kept seeing their faces as she walked the last few yards home in the cold drizzle. Al, her cheeks red and tearstained. Mrs. Glass, with a hopeful smile still painted on her face. And Suzannah, who'd had no expression at all. No hope, no anger, no disappointment. She was like a chalkboard that had been wiped clean.

Elizabeth paused on the front porch. There was no point in letting anyone see how upset she was. And there was no point in panicking, not yet. Mr. Glass could still come home tonight. Everything could still work out all right. *Please let it all be OK*, she pleaded silently.

She looked up at the darkening sky. In the distance thunder rolled. The radio had warned of blizzard conditions up north.

Elizabeth pushed open the door and took off her raincoat.

"There you are!" Mrs. Wakefield called from the living room. She and Mr. Wakefield were sitting on the couch, going through a pile of bills. "Are you soaked to the bone?"

"Just about."

"Dinner in half an hour," Mrs. Wakefield said.

Elizabeth was halfway up the stairs when something occurred to her. It was so obvious, she was surprised she hadn't thought of it sooner. Maybe her parents could help out the Glasses until Mr. Glass got back. It would mean telling them the whole truth, admitting that she'd taken the party money. Her parents would be furious with her. But if it meant that the Glasses could stay in their apartment, that would be a small price to pay.

She returned to the hallway. Her parents were deep in conversation on the couch, their backs to Elizabeth. Elizabeth swallowed. She wasn't used to admitting she'd made such a big mistake to her parents.

How would Jessica break it to them? she wondered. Jessica usually liked to butter them up a little when she had really bad news. But there wasn't time for that. And all the buttering up in the world wouldn't make it any easier to explain to her parents that their daughter was a thief.

Mr. Wakefield leaned back and rubbed his eyes. Elizabeth could see a calculator on the coffee table. "We'll be paying off these Christmas bills till next July," he muttered.

"Maybe we did go a little overboard this year," Mrs. Wakefield said quietly. "The next couple months will be a little tight."

Elizabeth leaned against the hallway wall and sighed. She had the feeling this wasn't a good time to be asking her parents for the kind of money she needed. And something else occurred to her. Would Elizabeth be getting Mrs. Glass into trouble if she told about the money? Mrs. Glass hadn't known it was stolen, of course. And it hadn't *really* been stolen, not exactly. But still . . .

"What's wrong, Elizabeth?"

Jessica came down the stairs. She was carrying her red notebook.

"I have a headache," Elizabeth said, rubbing her temples.

She pointed to Jessica's notebook. "Did you decide on a party?"

"Well, I decided we're going shopping tomorrow morning," Jessica said. "I'm hoping the solution will come to me in my dreams tonight."

"Me too," Elizabeth said wearily.

Jessica peered into the living room. "Are Mom and Dad busy?"

"I wouldn't bother them if I were you. I think they're talking about money."

"Perfect." Jessica strode into the living room. "Dad?" she said. "Are you busy tomorrow morning?"

Mr. Wakefield turned around. "I've got some last-minute shopping to do. Why?"

"I was wondering if you'd mind going by the bank first thing."

Elizabeth nearly swallowed her tongue. "Jess!" she hissed.

"And why would you want me to go by the bank, if you don't mind my asking?" Mr. Wakefield asked.

"For my money, of course."

Elizabeth rushed into the living room and grabbed Jessica's arm. "Jessica!" she said, grinning through clenched teeth. "You joker, you. I'm the banker in this family. Don't you bother about all that financial stuff—"

"Stop yanking on my sweater," Jessica complained. "You're stretching the arm."

"Come *on*, Jess," Elizabeth insisted. "Mom and Dad are really busy."

"Is there something I should know about?" Mr. Wakefield asked. "Because I seem to be totally lost."

"I just want to get my party money—" Jessica began.

"And you *will*, Jess," Elizabeth said firmly, pulling even harder on Jessica's sweater. "But it's my responsibility, and I want to take care of it."

"All right already!" Jessica cried. "Just let go of me!"

Elizabeth pulled with all her might, jerking Jessica into the hallway. She peeked back into the living room and gave her parents a sheepish grin.

"Sorry," she said. "Just some last-minute Christmas secrets."

"I hope we're surprised," Mrs. Wakefield said with a grin.

"Oh, I think you will be," Elizabeth replied grimly.

"Look what you did to my sleeve!" Jessica snapped when Elizabeth joined her in the hall. "You turned it into an ape arm! And why are you being so weird about the bank?"

Elizabeth slumped onto the bottom stair and sighed. She was tired. She was confused. She'd told so many lies, she didn't know where the lies ended and the truth began. She looked over at Jessica. How many times had Jessica been in a jam like this?

For a moment she considered telling her sister the truth. But why upset Jessica when Mr. Glass might still come through?

"What?" Jessica asked. "What are you looking at? My ape arm?"

"I was just thinking about all the times you've gotten yourself into trouble and how you always somehow manage to get out of it."

Jessica grinned. "Not without your help."

"How do you stand being you, Jess?" Elizabeth asked wearily. "Isn't it exhausting?"

Jessica draped her droopy sweater arm around Elizabeth's shoulder. "You're worried about the party, aren't you?" she said. "That's so sweet. But I don't want you to worry about a thing. I'll make this party a success if it's the last thing I do." She grinned. "Things always work out in the end."

"I hope so, Jess," Elizabeth said. "I really hope so."

Nine

The rain just wouldn't stop.

It was still beating against the window when Elizabeth awoke the next morning. She turned off her alarm clock and peeked out at the gloomy morning. At least the weather matched her mood.

She dressed quickly, careful to be quiet in the bathroom so she wouldn't wake Jessica. It was early to be going to the Glasses, but they didn't have a phone yet and it was the only way Elizabeth could find out what had happened with Mr. Glass.

Maybe he'd made it home safe and sound last night. She'd knock on the door and find the whole family having breakfast in the cozy, bright kitchen. They'd invite Elizabeth in for waffles, and after they were through, Mrs. Glass would take her aside and press crisp bills into Elizabeth's hand. "Thank you for your help," she'd say, and Elizabeth would know she'd done the right thing. She'd rush back home, give Jessica and the Unicorns the money, and by this evening, everyone would gather happily for a huge soccer-jazz-Hollywood-luau Christmas party. And at last she'd be able to start enjoying Christmas.

Anything is possible at Christmastime, Elizabeth told herself.

She frowned into the mirror. Her pimple had acquired additional territory and was now the size of Wyoming. Somehow, under the circumstances, it was hard to get her hopes up.

She read the note she'd prepared one last time:

> Jess—
>   Had to run a quick errand. Back soon. Don't worry about the money. It's all taken care of.
>
>   E.

Elizabeth taped the note to the mirror, the one place she could be certain Jessica would see it.

She stared at her own reflection. "Liar," she muttered accusingly, and then she was off.

*   *   *

Even before she talked to the Glasses, Elizabeth knew she was about to hear bad news. There was a car in front of the Glasses' apartment, a car Elizabeth recognized. It belonged to Connie from the shelter.

The door to the apartment was open. Connie was packing up a few odds and ends into a small cardboard box. She looked at Elizabeth and shook her head. "They're in the living room," she said.

Mrs. Glass was sitting on an overstuffed, battered suitcase, trying to force a broken lock to close. When she saw Elizabeth, she smiled. "You'd think I could get this thing to close, wouldn't you?"

Elizabeth knelt down next to her. With a grunt of effort, she managed to get the suitcase shut. Mrs. Glass kept smiling, but her lower lip was trembling.

"Did you hear anything?" Elizabeth asked gently.

She shook her head. "I was up all night. I kept shoveling change into that pay phone across the street, calling the highway patrol, hospitals, anyone I could think of." She rubbed her eyes. "It's just not like Carl not to get in touch with us. I know we don't have a phone, but he could have left a message at the shelter."

"Maybe he's snowed in," Elizabeth said. "Maybe he can't get to a phone."

"Maybe," Mrs. Glass said wearily.

Connie came into the room. "All set?"

"Let me get the girls." Mrs. Glass stood slowly. "I can't thank you enough for making room for us at the shelter, Connie."

"Well, it may be a little cramped," Connie said.

"Hey, it's a roof over our heads," Mrs. Glass said. "And in this weather, that's saying something."

"I'm ready," Al said. She trudged into the room, carrying a paper shopping bag. "Hi, Lisbet." With a sigh, she gazed around her. "Bye, 'partment. Bye, swing." Suddenly her eyes went wide. "We have to bring our Christmas tree, Mom!"

"Of course you can bring it," Connie said. "We'll find a nice sunny window for it at the shelter."

"Are you coming with us, Lisbet?"

Elizabeth shook her head. "I have something to do at home, Al. Maybe later."

"Let's load up, guys," Mrs. Glass said. "Elizabeth, would you mind getting Suzannah? She's in her bedroom."

Elizabeth found Suzannah sitting in the little

alcove in her room, reading a book.

"Is it time?" she asked without emotion.

Elizabeth nodded. "I'm really sorry, Suzannah. I wish I could make things all right."

Suzannah closed her book. "Could you hand me that bag?" she asked.

Elizabeth reached for the plastic bag on Suzannah's bed. Inside were a few neatly folded clothes, a hairbrush, and a little stuffed dog.

"I travel light," Suzannah said with a shrug. She set down her book and reached for the bag. Her eyes glistened, but her face was as still as stone. "I don't mind going back to the shelter so much," she said. "That doesn't matter. I just wish—" she choked back tears, "I just wish I knew if my dad was all right."

Elizabeth hugged her gently as her own eyes filled with tears. "He is," she said. "I'm sure of it."

Suzannah pulled away. She straightened her shoulders and headed out the door without looking back.

"Wait," Elizabeth said, pointing to the bookshelf. "What about your books?"

Suzannah shook her head. "It's too hard to concentrate at the shelter with all the noise. You can have them if you want."

Elizabeth picked up the tattered paperback

Suzannah had been reading. It was an Amanda Howard mystery, one she'd already read. She tucked it in her raincoat pocket. Somehow she just couldn't bear to see it left behind.

When Elizabeth got home, the house was filled with voices. She could hear Jessica in the family room talking to members of the planning committee. She could hear Mr. Wakefield and Steven in the living room arguing about how to string lights on the Christmas tree.

She looked into the kitchen. Mrs. Wakefield was unpacking Christmas ornaments from a large box on the table. Elizabeth thought of the little cardboard box Connie had been packing for the Glasses. All their belongings had fit into a battered suitcase, a couple of shopping bags, and a tiny box.

In the family room, Jessica and Lila were laughing. They wouldn't be for long, Elizabeth thought miserably. It was time. She had to go tell them there was no money. She'd ruined the Glasses' Christmas, and now she was about to ruin theirs.

She headed into the family room. Everyone was there, all the Unicorns.

The room fell silent. Elizabeth stood there, her raincoat dripping on the carpet. All eyes were on her.

"I have something to say," she said.

"No!" Jessica leaped up. "*I* have something to say!" Her eyes were dark with anger. "What have you done with the money?"

Elizabeth blinked. "You . . . you know?"

"I asked Dad about the deposit this morning." Jessica crossed her arms over her chest. "Only, it turns out there never *was* a deposit."

"Where is it, Elizabeth?" Lila exploded. "What have you done with it?"

"Do you realize how many cookies I baked to raise money for this party?" Ellen cried.

"Be quiet, everybody," Janet commanded. "I'm sure Elizabeth has a logical explanation for this. Don't you?"

Elizabeth gazed around the room. She couldn't tell them the truth. She'd made the Glasses miserable enough. What if she got them into even more trouble by revealing that Mrs. Glass had accepted stolen money?

"I . . . " Elizabeth's voice faded away. "I can't explain." She cast a hopeful glance at Jessica, but even her face was hard and angry.

"What do mean, you can't explain?" Tamara demanded. "We're talking about three hundred and eighty-six dollars, Elizabeth!"

"What did it do, just disappear?" Jessica cried.

Elizabeth felt her hands begin to tremble. "I'm

sorry," she whispered. "I really am. I guess I . . . I lost it." Tears spilled down her cheeks. "I'll pay you back, I promise I will."

"What are we supposed to do for a party?" Janet asked.

"You could still have a party," Elizabeth said.

"With no food? No entertainment? No decorations?" Lila demanded.

"But . . ." Elizabeth paused. Her words got lost. She tried again. "But Jessica hasn't even decided on a theme," she said lamely.

"It doesn't even matter now," Jessica cried. "There isn't going to *be* any party!" Her expression was hurt and confused. "I don't understand, Elizabeth. You're the responsible one. You're the one everyone counts on." Her voice wobbled. "How could let us all down this way? How could you let *me* down this way?" She brushed away a tear.

"I didn't mean to, Jess," Elizabeth sobbed. "It just happened. Sometimes things don't turn out the way you planned. I was just trying to help."

"Help *who*? You're not helping anyone. All you've done is ruin everything," Jessica cried, her face flushed with emotion. "I wish you weren't my sister, Elizabeth. I wish—I wish I'd never had a twin!"

The words struck like lightning. Elizabeth

sobbed again and ran from the room. She threw open the front door and fled into the rain. It didn't matter where she was going as long as she could run to a place where she couldn't hurt anyone else. The rain kept falling, and so did her tears.

At last, after she had cried until she felt numb, Elizabeth found herself at the outskirts of the Sweet Valley Mall. She wound her way through the long rows of cars, heading for the entrance without really knowing why—she didn't want to be around crowds of happy holiday shoppers. But she was tired and wet and cold and she wanted to sit down and sort out her thoughts.

Elizabeth trudged slowly through the mall until she came to the bright, glittery platform where Santa Claus sat on a throne molded of papier mâché and decorated with sparkles. A long line of children waited for the chance to sit on his lap and have their photos taken by a girl dressed as an elf.

Long ago, Elizabeth had stood in a line like that with Jessica, waiting to talk with Santa. The memory made her sad. In those days she had believed in Santa Claus. She'd believed, as Jessica still did, that in the end everything would always turn out all right.

Now she could see that Santa's beard was coming unglued from his right cheek and that his cuffs were frayed and a little dirty. And now she knew that everything did not always turn out all right in the end.

She stared at the twirling display of animated mechanical figures behind him. Life-sized elves waved jerkily. Angels with tinsel halos hung from steel wires connected to the ceiling, swaying in the air-conditioned breeze. A little plastic boy pounded on a plastic drum. From a speaker behind him, "The Little Drummer Boy" song played, but the mechanical figure had no sense of rhythm. *Pa-rum-pa-pum-pum, rum-pa-pum-pum.* She hated that song.

Elizabeth stood numbly, watching the glittering display wobble and bob through eyes brimming with tears. She had never felt so tired. Frantic last-minute shoppers rushed around her, but she was too weary to get out of their way. She felt like a rock in a fast-moving river.

She stared at the line of fidgeting children who waited for their turns to tell Santa their wishes. *I know what I wish*, Elizabeth thought as a tear trailed down her cheek. *I wish I'd never been born.*

She closed her eyes, swallowing a sob as more tears came, steady as the rain outside. Something inside her ached, a cold, hard pain that made her want to cry out loud. She had to get out of here. She didn't belong here with the happy crowds and the grinning drummer boy and the floating angels. She didn't belong anywhere.

She wiped her eyes with the back of her hand and spun around. The lights had suddenly dimmed. The crowd moved with heavy feet, like a slow-motion film. The carols faded. *Me and my drum . . .* came the song, but now it was just a tinny echo.

Elizabeth tried to move, but her feet weren't obeying. She heard a squeaky noise above her, like a rope through a pulley. She looked up and saw one of the angel mannequins slowly lowering to the ground.

What is going on here? Elizabeth wondered. She tried to turn away, but again her feet refused her orders.

The angel came closer and seemed to . . . wave. But, of course, that was impossible, Elizabeth told herself. The angel was just a prop, a lifeless mannequin with a tinfoil halo. Elizabeth blinked and looked again.

That was no angel. That was definitely a girl. A strange-looking girl, yes. A girl on a string, yes. But it was definitely a live girl.

"Give me a hand, would you?" the girl called.

Elizabeth closed her eyes, waiting for the fog

in her brain to clear. When she opened them, she saw that the girl had landed just inches in front of her. She was shaking silver glitter out of her long, dark braid. The flowing white gown was gone, replaced by jeans and a T-shirt.

"I don't suppose you've got a clue about how to unhook this sucker, do you?" the girl asked. She studied the wire harness under her arms, frowning.

"I—I have to go," Elizabeth said, the words nearly sticking in her throat.

"Hang on, hang on, you got a plane to catch or something?" said the girl. She unsnapped a buckle and eased her way out of the harness. Then she stuck out her hand and grabbed Elizabeth's. Elizabeth shook it. It was like shaking hands with a popsicle.

Elizabeth stared, first at the girl's hand. Then at the girl's face, as pale and translucent as a new moon. Then at the girl's clothes, her torn, shredded blue jeans, her Beatles tie-dye shirt, the peace-sign earrings dangling from her ears.

"What are you staring at?" the girl said irritably. Suddenly her huge gray eyes went wide. "Oh!" She reached up and pulled off the tinfoil halo still sitting at a cockeyed angle on her head. "Puh-lease," she said, looking it over skeptically. "*No*body wears these anymore."

"Wh—who are you?" Elizabeth whispered.

The girl put her arm around Elizabeth's shoulder. "I'm Laura," she said. She gazed around the cavernous room and let out a satisfied sigh. "It's groovy to finally meet you, Elizabeth."

Elizabeth blinked again. How did this girl know her name? It was *groovy* to meet her?

"How do you know my name?" she asked. "And what were you doing hanging from the ceiling, pretending to be an angel?"

"What do you mean, pretending?" Laura demanded. "I *am* an angel. In fact, Elizabeth, I'm your guardian angel."

Ten

"I've got to go," Elizabeth muttered. She tried to push past, but Laura reached for her shoulder and held firm. Her grip was amazingly strong.

"No way, Jose." Laura shook her head. "Rule number eight in the *Angel Trainee Handbook*. I can't let you out of my sight." She gazed over toward the food court. "Man, have I got a serious case of the munchies. You can really work up an appetite when you don't get any decent junk food for twenty-five years."

Elizabeth followed the direction of her gaze. The crowd of people still seemed to be moving in slow motion. The familiar mall sounds—the noisy crowd, the happy carols, the cries of children, the beeping of cash registers—had blurred to a soft murmur, like a rush of water.

"I have to go," Elizabeth said again.

"You think they've got any corn dogs here? I've had corn dogs on the brain since the late sixties." Laura shook her head regretfully. "Not that we don't get to eat. But the angel in charge of food is named Maurice. Very French. He doesn't approve of junk food."

Something had changed. Something terrible had happened. The whole world was out of focus. Elizabeth put her palm to her forehead. Could it be she had a fever? One thing she did know—she had to get out of there. She closed her eyes and, with all her will, tried to push past Laura toward the exit. But she couldn't move. Her feet seemed to be glued to the floor.

"This is crazy," Elizabeth said, holding her head in both hands. "This is insane. This is impossible. I . . . I can't even move my feet."

"Oh, sorry about that, chief," Laura said. She pointed a finger at Elizabeth's legs.

Elizabeth moved a foot forward tentatively.

"Don't go running off until I explain a few things," Laura advised.

Elizabeth stared at the frozen figures of people around her. They were now as still as statues. A little girl sat on Santa's lap, her mouth open in silent laughter. A woman peered into her shopping bag, motionless.

"What's happened?" Elizabeth whispered.

"No big deal," Laura said. "I can undo it all with a snap of my fingers."

"I'm losing my mind," Elizabeth said. "I'm losing my mind, and you've already lost yours." She paused. "Or maybe I'm just having a dream. A very strange dream."

"Liz, Liz, Liz, there's no point in getting upset. By the way, do you mind if I call you Liz? I know Jessica calls you Lizzie sometimes, so I figured you'd be cool with it. Liz. I like the sound of it. It makes me think, you know, Liz Taylor, Richard Burton. True love. Big diamonds. Eternal romance."

"Not eternal," Elizabeth said automatically. "Richard Burton is dead."

"Dead, huh? Funny, I haven't seen him around," Laura said. "But then, you can't meet everyone. Not even in eternity. I mean, who's got the time? Besides, I'm not exactly a social butterfly like Jessica."

Elizabeth stared at her. "How do you know Jessica?"

"I know everyone you know," Laura said as she wandered over to a shop window to examine a display of string bikinis. "I know Steven and Jessica and your mom and dad and Amy and Lila—you name it. Oh, and Suzannah and Al, of course. How could I forget them? They're the reason you're in such a major funk." She pressed her nose to the window. "Do chicks really wear these things in public?"

This has to be a dream, Elizabeth thought. *I'm either having an insane dream, or I'm just plain hallucinating.* "I have to get out of here," she repeated, taking a couple of stumbling steps toward the exit.

"Come on, it's cool," Laura said, falling in beside her. "Stick with me. Before you know it, we'll be best friends."

"I don't have any friends. Not anymore," Elizabeth said bitterly. "And I'm pretty sure I don't want to start over again with you. I don't think I could ever have a long-term friendship with a hallucination."

"Hallucination, huh?" Laura said, sounding amused. "That's what you think?" She shook her head. "Anyway, you're nuts if you think you don't have friends."

Elizabeth stopped in her tracks. The tears welled up again as she recalled all the angry faces that morning. Especially Jessica's. The tears spilled over and ran down her cheeks.

"Please don't cry, OK?" Laura said. "I'm really bad with the crying scene. I mean, I flunked 'Helping with Heavy Emotions' twice, Liz." She wrung her hands. "Please, anything but crying. Hit me, throw things, kick a dog.

I'm good with the physical stuff."

Elizabeth sobbed, a deep, hurting sob that shook her whole body. She had to be alone, free of this crazy girl she was imagining. Maybe she could run away. Yes. Running away. Far away. Why not? In a dream you could do anything. She could take a bus, maybe—

"Snap out of it, kid, would you? I mean, how many people get to meet their very own guardian angel?" Laura fumbled in her jeans pocket and retrieved a mangled piece of pink tissue. "Here." She shoved it into Elizabeth's hand.

Elizabeth stared at it blankly. "Please," she said, sobbing softly, "just go away and leave me alone. Just disappear or whatever it is you do."

"Geez, I know the Kleenex is a little gross, but it's the only one I've got. It's been in my pocket for a quarter of a century. That's practically an antique, you know." She looked down at her well-worn jeans. "It was cool of them to give me back my original clothes for this trip, don't you think? Usually you have to wear the whole white-robe thing because that's what people expect. But I told them no, my girl Liz would be more comfortable if I just dressed normally. Plus, man, I missed my jeans."

For a moment, Elizabeth forced herself to stare into Laura's huge eyes. They were soft gray like a misty mirror. Strange eyes, sad and wistful and content at the same time. Despite the wisecracking, there was an inner light there too. Was it actually possible? Was it even remotely possible that this wasn't a dream?

Elizabeth looked around at the hundreds of shoppers, still frozen and silent. *Definitely a dream,* she decided. Reality just never ever got this weird.

"Laura, you seem like a really nice hallucination, but I need to be alone right now," Elizabeth said, mustering what little strength she had. "Do you maybe have some . . . some dream parents who might be waiting for you? Some hallucinated friends who could take care of you? Take you home? It's Christmas Eve, you know."

"Du-uh. I guess that would explain the big fat guy over there with the long white beard and the plastic reindeer." She looked curiously at Elizabeth. "So, I'm just a dream, huh? Or maybe an escaped lunatic?"

"A little of both," Elizabeth said sniffling. "But that's OK. I'm feeling kind of loony myself at the moment."

Laura laughed heartily. "I like you, Liz. I like you fine." She pointed to the tissue Elizabeth was clutching. "Now blow."

Elizabeth blew her nose obediently. Suddenly she was too weary to argue.

"Come on," Laura said, motioning toward the mall doors. "Time to hit the road. We have places to go, people to see. Besides, if I hear one more chorus of 'The Little Drummer Boy,' I'll gag."

"You want to leave?" Elizabeth asked.

"It's time," Laura said.

"Where do you think we're supposed to go?" Elizabeth asked.

"We're going where you wanted to go," Laura answered mysteriously. "I'm going to make your wish come true. That's what this is all about."

Elizabeth managed a sad smile. It would be nice to have a wish come true even if this were just a dream.

Laura stopped at the doors that lead out of the mall, and held out her hand. Her smile was sweet. "Come on, Liz. Trust me on this one. If I'm just a dream, then what do you have to lose? You'll wake up eventually."

Elizabeth looked through the big glass doors. She could see the rain had stopped. A cold fog, thick as cotton, quilted the ground. The parking lot, the trees, the hills of Sweet Valley beyond were all completely hidden. She looked back over her shoulder. "Are you just going to leave all these people frozen like this?" Elizabeth waved her hand toward the throngs of motionless shoppers.

Laura smiled. "You *are* a goody-goody, aren't

you?" She snapped her fingers. Suddenly the entire mall sprang to life as if a photograph had suddenly become real. "One of the few things I can do pretty well," Laura said with satisfaction. "I've got the freeze-frame thing down cold. Now, do we go forward or not?"

"Forward where?" Elizabeth asked.

"Forward to make your wish come true. Haven't you been paying attention?"

Elizabeth swallowed. She thought of her family at home, of the sugar cookies Jessica would be burning and the cockeyed angel Steven would place on the top of the tree.

Then she thought of the disappointment in Jessica's eyes that morning, of the ruined party, of Todd, of her angry friends. She thought of Suzannah and Al packing up their belongings, staring wistfully at the home they had grown to love but couldn't have.

She had ruined Christmas for so many people, and nothing she could do could make it all right again. This dream was strange and unsettling, but it was still better than reality. The truth was, she didn't want to wake up.

Elizabeth reached for Laura's icy fingers, and together they stepped out into a cold, gray world.

Eleven

They walked for a while in silence. There was nothing to see but parked cars, and nothing much to hear. The fog had hidden the world from view. Even Laura, just a few inches away, was a vague shadow in the mist. Elizabeth clung tightly to her hand, but no matter how hard she squeezed, it remained as cold as stone.

"This is crazy," Elizabeth said, thinking aloud. "We can't see a thing. Why would I dream fog?"

"Has to be this way for a while," Laura explained. "Until all the changes can be made."

"Changes?"

"It's a very complicated job, rewriting history," Laura explained. "They tell me it's a miracle that it works at all. Ha ha. Get it? Miracle? Anyway, when they're ready, they'll get rid of the fog."

"My wish wasn't all that complicated," Elizabeth said. "All I wanted was for Suzannah and Al and Mrs. Glass to be all right, and the money not to be missing, and Todd—" Elizabeth stopped, feeling overwhelmed.

"Actually, you wanted *not to be born*," Laura corrected. "That *is* complicated. You'll see just how complicated it can be." Laura stopped and rested her hands on her hips. "Still, I wish they'd hurry up, because I am totally lost. Unfortunately, I have a lousy sense of direction. Pitiful. I flunked 'Navigation' three times. But I thought I had the map of Sweet Valley down cold—the mall, the beach, the school. Now I don't know where I am."

"We're still in the parking lot of the mall," Elizabeth said. "Over there's the bus stop—" she pointed to her right, "and up ahead is a big oak tree on the corner."

"If you say so."

"Of course I say so. I should know. Jessica's dragged me to the mall enough."

"I see a light up ahead," Laura said.

Elizabeth squinted. "I see it, too. That's the frozen-yogurt place."

"Frozen yogurt? I like yogurt, but why would anyone freeze the stuff?"

"It's like ice cream," Elizabeth explained. "Only it's better for you."

"Cool. Let's go get some," Laura said. "Follow me."

"Wait a minute. Why am I following you? I'm the dreamer here. You're just the one getting dreamed. I should be telling *you* where to go."

Laura snapped her fingers. "Oh, so you're in an I'm-In-Charge-Here phase. My instructor Clarence told me this would happen. It comes just after the Stunned-and-Disbelieving phase." Laura chewed on her thumbnail. "Man, I wish he'd let me bring my cheat sheet. I had the map and itinerary all memorized, but now I'm not so sure. Were we supposed to start at this yogurt place?"

"That does it," Elizabeth said firmly. "I'm going to some other dream."

"I don't think so, Liz." Laura shook her head. "Look, maybe we should get past this whole dream idea of yours. It's getting to be kind of a pain. I guess I need to convince you of who I am."

"I know who you are," Elizabeth said patiently. "You're my guardian angel. And I'm the tooth fairy. Good-bye." Elizabeth started to walk away, but Laura caught up to her in the blink of an eye.

"Please go away," Elizabeth said. "It's not that I want to wake up. I don't. And it's not that I don't like you. It's just that if I have to be in a dream, I'd rather be in a dream that involves sunny beaches and warm sunshine. Or at least a dream where . . ." Elizabeth swallowed the lump in her throat. "A dream where I haven't screwed up everything in my life." Suddenly a wave of sadness washed over her again.

"Oh, man, not the crying again!" Laura moaned. "You sure can blubber. I don't remember this in your file. I know your whole P-3 by heart, and blubbering was not mentioned once."

Elizabeth wiped the tears from her eyes. "P-3?" she repeated.

"Personality Problems Profile. *Elizabeth can be very self-critical. Occasionally she takes on more responsibility than is age-appropriate. She can be stubborn and exhibits a tendency toward self-righteousness.*"

"I am not self-righteous!" Elizabeth said defensively. "I am—" She stopped midsentence. Why was she arguing with a hallucination? She shrugged. "Maybe I am a little self-righteous."

"Sure you are. You're a major goody-goody. I used to hate nice girls like you. You give bad girls like me a complex." Laura gazed toward the sky. "Of course," she added in a sincere voice, "since then I've seen the error of my ways."

Elizabeth took a deep breath and blew her nose again. Laura gave her an awkward pat on the back, then grabbed her arm. "Come on. To the frozen-yogurt stand," she said, practically dragging Elizabeth along.

"Here we are," Laura announced as they reached the door a few minutes later. "It's all coming back to me now. Clarence *did* say something about an ice cream parlor. Ice cream, frozen yogurt, close enough. Right? Clarence isn't exactly up on all the latest trends. Either way, it's stop number one."

Laura opened the door to a tiny shop Elizabeth had been in a hundred times before. She even recognized the tired-looking old couple working behind the counter. The only customers in the place were a young mother and her two small daughters. Packages were piled around their table, as if they'd just finished their last-minute shopping.

"You'd better order quickly if you want anything," Elizabeth said to Laura, clearing her throat. "They'll be closing soon." She turned to the old woman behind the counter. "Hi, Mrs. Lambert. I'm the person having this dream. I hope you don't mind."

The old woman didn't answer. She just kept wiping the counter with an old rag, humming a Christmas carol to herself.

"She can't hear you," Laura said.

"It's *my* dream," Elizabeth said. "She can hear me if I say she can hear me."

"Oh, yeah?" Laura folded her arms. "Great. If you're so sure this is a dream, go ahead. Get her to answer you. Go on, give it your best shot."

"Hello!" Elizabeth yelled to the old woman.

"I don't see her answering," Laura said with a smirk.

"Hey! Mrs. Lambert!" Elizabeth shouted.

"Keep trying," Laura suggested, grinning. She sauntered past the refrigerated glass case, scanning the flavors. "Man, this stuff looks great. Strawberry-cheesecake frozen yogurt! Triple-chocolate devil's-food delight!" She shook her head. "Better skip that one, under the circumstances." Suddenly her expression darkened. "The things I've missed out on," she said softly.

"Hey! Excuse me! My friend and I would like to order some frozen yogurt!" Elizabeth practically screamed. The old woman kept wiping the counter. Her husband began counting out the money in the register. The young mother and her children went on eating without even looking up.

"Don't waste your time trying to order," Laura said. With a wicked grin, she spun around and marched over to the little girls' table. The mother and daughters ignored Laura completely.

With a sly wink at Elizabeth, Laura dipped her finger into one of the sundaes. When she pulled it out, it was coated with yogurt and chocolate sauce. Elizabeth gasped, waiting for the mother's outraged response. But she just continued to eat, staring off into space wearily.

The little girl frowned at her sundae. "Mommy," she muttered, "there's a hole in my yogurt."

"Don't be silly, Maggie," the woman said.

Laura licked the frozen yogurt off her finger. She was inches away from the little girl, yet no one seemed to be aware of her.

Laura sat down in a booth and motioned for Elizabeth to join her. "Not bad," she commented. "But I think I'll stick to ice cream. I'm kind of old-fashioned about these things."

Elizabeth settled into the booth uneasily. "They act like they can't hear us or see us, but they noticed it when you ate that yogurt," she said. "Why would I dream these things? They don't make sense. Also, that was a little gross."

"What?"

"You stuck your finger in that little girl's sundae."

Laura frowned. "You're saying that was rude?"

"I'm saying that was disgusting." Elizabeth shook her head again. "But the little girl definitely noticed that someone had made a hole in her sundae."

"Come on, Liz. You're supposed to be such a brain," Laura taunted. "Figure it out. They can't see us or hear us. But we're obviously here."

Laura's eyes fell on the napkin dispenser. She grabbed a handful, rolled them into a ball, and applied some saliva for good measure. Then she tossed it at the nearest girl's head.

"Stop it, Tonya!" Maggie cried indignantly. "First you poke my sundae. Now you throw spitballs at me!"

"Girls, I've had a rough day and it's Christmas Eve. Can't you give me a moment's peace?" their mother demanded.

The little girls fell into an uneasy silence.

"Ma'am," Elizabeth interrupted, "I think you should know it really wasn't Maggie's fault. My friend here—" She paused. The woman was licking her ice-cream cone, still completely oblivious. "Ma'am?" Elizabeth repeated more loudly.

"Watch this," Laura said gleefully. She tore off the end of a wrapped straw. "Ten points if I hit her mouth while it's open. Twenty points for a nostril."

"What is *wrong* with you?" Elizabeth cried.

Laura shrugged. Her impish grin was a lot like Jessica's when she got into trouble. "Sorry," she said sheepishly. "I have antisocial tendencies."

"That's an understatement."

"I was just trying to prove a point, Liz. You might as well get used to it, because as long as we're together, you're going to get ignored." She grinned. "After a while I bet you'll think it's kind of a trip. We can eavesdrop on the most interesting conversations. We can say outrageous things without getting into trouble. Here, listen up." She turned to the old woman behind the counter. "Hey, lady," she called, "I just flew in from Mars and I am absolutely famished. Do you know where I can get a nice, juicy humanoid steak?"

The old woman examined a spot on the counter as if she hadn't heard a word Laura had said.

"See?" Laura rubbed her palms together. "Man, I love this. It's perfect for a slightly re-formed juvenile delinquent like me. You, I'm not so sure about. You may be too nice to enjoy the opportunities."

"I don't understand." Elizabeth rubbed her temples. She had a terrible headache. Maybe she really was sick. What kind of a dream was this? It was going on so long. Everything seemed so weirdly real. Fear began to gnaw at her. "I've never had a dream like this," she muttered.

"Boy, that's the truth, Lizzie. Your dreams are all there in your P-3 file. And a boring bunch of dreams they are, too."

"OK, I'm ready to wake up now," Elizabeth announced. "Right now. I'm ready. Wake up, Elizabeth!"

Laura put her hand on Elizabeth's. It was cold as death. The look in Laura's eyes was suddenly serious, even sad. "It's not going to be that easy, Elizabeth. See, you're not asleep. You're not dreaming. And that means you're not going to wake up."

"I . . . I want this dream to end," Elizabeth said.

"Liz, Liz, Liz." Laura shook her head sadly. "You gotta watch out what you wish for. See, you aren't dreaming, because the truth is, Liz, you don't even exist. Not to any of these people, not in *this* Sweet Valley. To them you're nothing. No one. Not even a memory."

"But I *am* here!" Elizabeth protested. "Maybe they can't see me or hear me, but I can touch them. I could throw spitballs like you, or steal a bite of their frozen yogurt just like you did."

"No, you can't," Laura said flatly. "I can do those things because, see, *I* really exist. *I'm* an angel. You, on the other hand . . . well, you're just a *possibility*."

Elizabeth felt her heart throbbing. She twisted around in her chair and reached a shaky hand out to touch the head of the little girl seated behind her. Her fingers lowered, lowered, till they were just inches away from the girl's brown hair.

She lowered her hand still farther.

Her fingers kept going, right through the little girl's head, as if her hand weren't even there. As if her hand were made of nothing more than fog.

Twelve

Just then something inside Elizabeth snapped. "Go away!" she screamed. "Go away and leave me alone!" She leaped from the booth and ran out the door, ignoring Laura's cries.

Outside, the fog was even thicker. She tore at it with her hands as if she could clear a path. She didn't know where she was, and she didn't know where she was going. That didn't really matter as long as she could get far, far away from Laura.

You're invisible. You don't even exist. I'm your guardian angel. The words swirled around in her head, dense as the fog. *You're just a possibility.* She rounded a corner, running faster now, the sound of her frantic footsteps swallowed up in the mist. She turned to see if Laura was following her. When she turned back she saw two boys in front of her hauling a Christmas tree. It was too late for her to stop. She was running too fast.

"Look out!" Elizabeth shouted. She stuck out her hands to cushion the impact, but they met no resistance. She flowed through one of the boys. Right through him. Suddenly she was skidding to a stop on the other side of him, looking at his back as he walked away.

"Man, that was weird," the boy said.

"What?" asked his friend.

"I just had this weird, creepy feeling all of a sudden." The boy shivered and looked nervously over his shoulder.

His friend nodded. "Everything's creepy in this fog."

Elizabeth felt a cold shiver run down her spine as Laura's words came back to her. *You don't even exist. You're just a possibility.*

The boys with the tree gradually disappeared into the fog. The only evidence they'd existed was the carpet of pine needles on the ground. Elizabeth knelt down and tried to scoop up a handful. The needles remained undisturbed. And yet she could see them. She could even smell their familiar cool, sweet scent.

They were real. The boys were real. The sidewalk and the fog and the fear in her heart were real. She *had* to be real, too . . . didn't she?

"Man, you can boogie, girl!"

Elizabeth jumped. Out of nowhere, Laura appeared before her as if the fog were a curtain she could open and close at will.

"You and I need to have a talk," Laura said breathlessly. "Try that again and they just might pull me off your case, know what I'm saying? There's no telling who you might end up with next. Trust me. I'm a lot more laid-back than some of the trainees."

"Am I delirious?" Elizabeth whispered. "I mean, I *did* have a headache before, and that could explain—"

"Liz, Liz, Liz," Laura said impatiently. "Are you dense or what? According to your file, you're a brain, but I'm starting to have my doubts. Look. I'm going to try this one more time, slow and simple." She fished around in her pocket. "See this?" She held up a little plastic name tag for Elizabeth to see.

Elizabeth gazed at the pin.

HELLO, MY NAME IS LAURA.
PLEASE BE PATIENT WITH ME. I AM A TRAINEE.

"So?" she said. "Are you training at Burger Buddy or something?"

"I'm training," Laura replied, "but not to fix

burgers. I fix souls, Liz." Laura stuffed the tag back in her pocket. "I'm supposed to wear that thing, but I'd feel like such a dork, you know? I mean, puh-leeze! 'Hello, my name is Laura, and I'll be your angel today.' I may be a trainee, but I do have some dignity."

"Laura, please," Elizabeth pleaded. "I need some answers. I'm really starting to worry I'm going crazy, so stop kidding around, OK?"

Laura stopped walking. She looked Elizabeth straight in the eyes. "I'm not kidding, Liz. I'm dead serious." She laughed. "Dead serious, get it? OK, OK, so you're not in the mood." She cleared her throat. "Look, I know you're a logical person, so let's take the evidence. I appear out of nowhere, hanging from a string in a mall, right?"

Elizabeth nodded slowly.

"I throw a spitball at someone and she can't see me, right?"

Again Elizabeth nodded.

"I know everything about you. I know about your fight with Todd. I know about that typo in the *Sixers*. I know about Suzannah and Jess and that zit on your chin and the fact that you can't tell a joke to save your life—"

"I can *so* tell jokes," Elizabeth protested.

Laura shook her head regretfully. "Sorry, Liz. You always blow the punch lines. But I digress.

The point is, add up all this stuff, and what have you got?"

"A very, very strange dream."

"Close, but no cigar. You've got me, your very own personal angel." Laura turned a corner, dragging Elizabeth along with her. "And do you know why I'm here?"

"To drive me insane?"

Laura made a loud noise like a game-show buzzer. "Sorry, you're incorrect once again, Liz baby. I am here to grant your wish."

Elizabeth sighed. What had she ever wished for? To make things right with Jessica and the others, to fix things up for Suzannah and her family . . . But it was too late for those wishes to come true. "I never wished for anything," she said. "Not anything that could come true now."

Laura made the buzzer sound. "Wrong again! You wished you had never been born. I distinctly heard you say it while I was swinging from the ceiling, listening to that obnoxious rum-pa-pa-pum number for the hundredth time."

They paused at a street corner. Laura squeezed Elizabeth's fingers in her icy hand.

"So they're not ninety-eight point six," Laura said defensively, noticing Elizabeth glancing down at her hand. "You try being dead for a few years and see how perky you feel. Besides, you're not one to complain. I'm the only person you can touch at all." She turned her head right, then left, peering into the soupy fog. "Now, before we get this show on the road, let's get the true confessions out of the way."

"What show? I'm not going anywhere with you."

"You have no choice, Liz." Laura's eyes went wide and she lowered her voice. "Why, I possess powers beyond your wildest dreams!"

"Really?"

"No, but I thought I'd give it a shot." Laura fingered one of her earrings. "What I need to confess, Liz, is that I'm not exactly your top-of-the-line angel trainee. I have what you might call bad study skills."

"So you're telling me you actually study to become an angel?"

"Hey, I've been studying since the late sixties," Laura cried. "This stuff isn't easy."

Elizabeth stared at Laura doubtfully. "Does everyone take so long to learn?"

Laura tilted her chin. "If you must know, I was in the remedial class. Certain very uncool teachers who had it in for me claimed I was a disruptive influence."

"And why was that?"

"Because I was a disruptive influence." Laura

shrugged. "But hey, that's old news. Here I am at long last, and you and I are going to have a groovy time."

"And then what?" Elizabeth asked. "Let me guess—you get your wings?"

"I know it's a cliché, but my boss is very traditional."

The stoplight changed to green. Laura screwed up her face, a look of determination on her pale features. "Let's see," she muttered. If that way's north, then which way's west?" She nudged Elizabeth in the arm. "You know where the Big Dipper is by any chance?"

Elizabeth crossed her arms over her chest. "Where are we going? Were you planning a little intergalactic travel, maybe?"

"No need for that," Laura said. "Sweet Valley will do just fine." She let out a sigh. "I guess we'll just have to give it our best try. Hang on to my hand and hope for the best, OK? I'm going to fly us."

Elizabeth rolled her eyes. "Great. Will there be an in-flight movie?"

"You have a sarcastic streak in you, Liz, did anyone ever tell you that? Remind me to add that to your P-3. Now, before we go, two more confessions." Laura sighed. "I mean, I feel like you should know the real me, since I already know all about you."

"Go for it."

"Confession one. I changed my name to Pussywillow for six months back in 1968, but it was just a stage I was going through."

"And?"

"Prepare for takeoff," Laura warned. She took a step forward. A cool breeze began to blow. Another step, and the wind picked up force. Elizabeth's hair whipped in her eyes. The fog swirled around them like a cyclone.

"Laura?" Elizabeth had to shout to be heard above the roar of the wind. "What was confession two?"

"I flunked flyer's ed." Laura squeezed Elizabeth's hand tightly and took a deep breath. "Three times."

Thirteen

"AHHHHHHHHHH!"

Elizabeth hurtled through the sky, screaming. Hundreds of feet below her, the world of Sweet Valley raced by. Color swirled and blurred and faded to gray. She spun around and found herself staring up into a blanket of dark clouds. She screamed again.

"Don't worry, relax!" Laura shouted over Elizabeth's screams. "I mean, you're not going to get killed or anything."

Elizabeth closed her eyes, shutting out the twisting, spinning world. Suddenly they came to a stop. She realized with a start that she was standing.

Slowly Elizabeth opened her eyes and waited for her stomach to catch up with the rest of her.

Laura was still holding her hand. Laura's face looked even whiter than usual, but she had a big, satisfied grin on her face. Wisps of hair that had come loose from her braid hung in her eyes.

"Far out!" she exclaimed. "Some trip, huh? And a pretty smooth landing, if I do say so myself."

Elizabeth looked around, feeling dazed and dizzy. The fog was gone. Above her a movie marquee flickered. "What just happened?" she asked, her voice quaking.

Laura spun around and giggled. "I'll tell you what just happened. We boogied down in a major way."

"Tell me again. Only this time, try not to get so technical, OK?"

"And the flight instructor said I couldn't pilot a paper airplane!" Laura exclaimed. She tilted her head back and gazed at the clouds. "Take *that*, Amelia! A perfect landing, right in the—" Her eyes fell on the marquee. "Wait a minute. What is this? A movie theater?"

"Over in the east end of town, I think," Elizabeth said uncertainly. "But how could that be? We were way over by the mall—"

"How could that be? How could that be?" Laura's voice rose an octave. She slapped herself on the forehead. "I'll tell you how that could be.

I'm an idiot, that's how. I totally lost concentration." She pointed to the marquee. "Look at that, will you? Look what's playing."

"An old movie, I know. They always play old movies here. The tickets are only two dollars."

"It's a Sophia Loren movie, Liz!" Laura exploded. "Can you believe it?"

"Well, it does seem like they could at least be playing a Christmas movie," Elizabeth conceded. "You know, something like *White Christmas*. Or *It's a Wonderful Life*. My mom loves that one."

Laura walked over to the ticket-seller's booth and pounded her head against the glass. The old man selling tickets looked up from the money he was counting, a quizzical expression on his face.

"Laura, you fool," Laura moaned. "Sophia *Rizzo*, not Sophia Loren."

"What are you talking about?"

"I was supposed to take you to see Sophia Rizzo," Laura said apologetically. "But me with my lousy sense of direction, me, flunkee of the century, what do I do? I take you to see a movie star instead." Her shoulders slumped. "Amelia was right. In the skies I'm a dangerous weapon. I just can't seem to keep my concentration."

Elizabeth touched her gently on the arm. "Don't feel bad, Laura. I'm sure you can learn to fly if you—" She groaned. "Wait a minute. What am I saying? I'm trying to console a girl because she can't *fly*?"

"How do you think you got here? By camel?"

Good question. Elizabeth pushed the question into the same part of her brain that she was pushing all the other impossible questions. "Why did you want me to see Sophia Rizzo?" she asked instead.

"Long story. You'll see soon enough." Laura threw back her shoulders and took a deep breath. "I guess we should give this another shot, huh? This time I'll concentrate. See, that's the trick— you have to think hard about where you want to go. Unless, hey—" She held up her index finger. "I don't suppose you want to take in a flick while we're here? It's not like we'd have to pay for tickets. We can just walk right on in."

"Laura! We can't do that."

Laura's face dropped. "Are you going to be this much of a downer the whole trip? Get real, Liz. It's not like they can cart us off to jail. I'm an angel, and you're just a possibility. How would they bust us?"

"I'm not going in without paying."

"I *told* them we were a bad match back when they first assigned me to you," Laura said, sighing. "You haven't got a troublemaking bone in your body."

Elizabeth gave a rueful laugh. "I've caused plenty of trouble," she said quietly. "Plenty."

"That reminds me," Laura said. "Sophia." She held out her hand. "Come on, let's give this another try."

Elizabeth took a step back. "Wherever we're going, how about if we just walk? I really don't want to fly again. Not like that."

"Backseat flyer," Laura muttered.

The farther they walked, the more uneasy Elizabeth became. There was something different about everything, something she couldn't quite put her finger on.

She shivered. Although the fog had at last cleared away, the sun was still hidden behind a bank of threatening gray clouds. A faded plastic snowman hung from one of the streetlamps, waving back and forth in the wind. Here and there tired-looking wreaths hung from shop windows, but everything seemed to have a staleness about it, as if no one really wanted to be reminded of the holiday.

"It seems different here somehow," Elizabeth said as they turned a corner. "The east side has always been a little seedy, but it looks worse than ever today."

Laura nodded. "Everything will seem a little off,

even familiar things. They tell me there are millions of little changes involved in something like this. You change one thing and an endless number of other changes have to be made. Everything is tied together, you know, sometimes in ways you'd never understand. They call it the Sweater Effect. You know how it is—you start yanking just one little loose thread on the sleeve of your sweater, and pretty soon you can unravel the whole thing."

Elizabeth looked at Laura suspiciously. "The Sweater Effect? Give me a break."

Laura shrugged. "Look, all I can tell you is what my teachers taught me. Albert explained the whole thing to me.

S E = I Y squared. Sweater Effect equals the number of Interactions times the number of Years on earth squared."

"Whatever you say, Laura," Elizabeth replied, shaking her head. "I think maybe I'll just try to find a phone now."

"And who would you call, exactly?"

"I don't know," Elizabeth admitted. "My mom, maybe, to tell her not to worry. Maybe a psychiatrist for you. For me too, actually."

"Trust me on this, Liz. Your mom's not worried." Suddenly Laura stopped. She grabbed Elizabeth's arm and pointed. "Next stop. Over there, on the corner."

"It's Sophia!" Elizabeth cried. "And her mom!"

"I was starting to think we'd never find them," Laura muttered.

A wave of relief rushed over Elizabeth. It felt good to see someone she knew. Whether this was a nightmare or actually some strange, twisted version of reality, Sophia might be able to clear it up. "I'm going to go talk to her," Elizabeth said firmly.

"Oh, really?" Laura asked mockingly.

"Hey, Sophia! Over here!" Elizabeth called, but Sophia didn't answer.

Elizabeth dashed down the street, leaving Laura behind. But as she got closer, she realized there was something very different about Sophia and her mother, something that sent currents of fear buzzing through her whole body.

Sophia's brown curls hung limply around her face, and her mouth was set in a dark scowl. She and her mother were both wearing torn, faded, secondhand clothes. One of Mrs. Rizzo's shoes had a broken heel that was barely staying on.

"Sophia," Elizabeth called again loudly.

Sophia didn't respond. She and her mother were having a heated argument about something. When her mother reached over to touch her shoulder, Sophia shook it off angrily. "Why should we go, Mama?" she snapped. "Why?"

"Because he's your brother, Sophia," her mother said in halting English. "Because it's Christmas Eve, and he's your brother."

Laura caught up with Elizabeth, panting heavily. "Cool it with the hundred-yard dashes, would you?" she complained. She fanned her face with her hand. "Man, am I out of shape. Of course," she reminded herself, "I'm also dead. I haven't done much actual physical exercise in a while."

"What's wrong with Sophia?" Elizabeth demanded. "I called her, but she won't answer."

"They were right about one thing in your P-3. You *are* stubborn, Liz. How many times do I have to remind you you're not real?"

"All right. Whatever you say," Elizabeth said impatiently. "Tell me this instead. Why do both of them look so sad?"

Sophia and her mother paused in front of a small grocery store with a tattered green awning over the door. But just as Sophia put her hand on the doorknob, the shopkeeper, a graying woman with a deeply lined face, opened the door and poked out her head. "We're closed," she snapped.

"But I just saw someone go inside," Sophia's mother protested in her heavy Italian accent. "Not more than two seconds ago."

"We're closed for you," the woman said sharply. "You and your no-good, shoplifting brat."

"But—I—I—"

"Your food's rotten, anyway!" Sophia shouted.

The door slammed shut. Sophia and her mother turned away slowly. Sophia had a defiant look pasted on her face, but her mother's dark eyes glistened with tears. They hurried back down the street without another word, as if they were both pretending nothing had happened.

"Why would anyone treat Sophia that way?" Elizabeth cried. "I know her. She would never shoplift!"

"Well, there are worse crimes," Laura said, peering into the grocery-store window.

Sophia and her mother crossed the street, heading toward a large brick building with a tall, barbed-wire fence around the yard. "That's the reform school," Elizabeth told Laura. "Why are they going there?"

"Tony's there," Laura said in a matter-of-fact voice. "He's been in all year."

"Sophia's brother?" Elizabeth cried. "That can't be! I mean, I know he used to get into trouble for stealing. And he got into fights at Sweet Valley High a lot, but that was a long time ago."

"I remember a doozy of a fight with Steven," Laura said.

Elizabeth gave her a sidelong glance. *"You* remember? How could you possibly remember? You don't even know Steven." Then Elizabeth held up her hands. "Forget it. Never mind. That's all in my file, too, right?"

Elizabeth followed Sophia and her mother to the front gatehouse, where a guard asked them for ID. Elizabeth reached for her wallet.

"What's that for?" Laura asked.

"They're checking IDs."

"Liz, people who don't exist don't require a lot of identification."

They followed Sophia and her mother inside through the grim steel gates. The room beyond was nearly empty, except for a long green table with chairs on either side. Sophia and her mother took their seats quietly, as if they'd been there many times before. After a few minutes another barred door opened at the other end of the room, and Tony appeared, escorted by a guard. He dropped down into a chair across from his mother and sister without a word.

"I don't understand this," Elizabeth said again, wringing her hands. "My father helped Tony get counseling. He's been doing much better at school. Everything's been going so well for them. Sophia's mom is—"

"Not without you, Liz," Laura said solemnly,

cutting her off. "Without you there to befriend Sophia when she was an outcast, her reputation got worse and worse. And Tony got into so many fights defending his mom and sister that he ended up here."

Elizabeth felt a shiver travel up her spine. "This isn't real," she whispered. "None of this is real. Sophia is a happy, popular girl with a nice big brother and a wonderful mother."

"Oh, really?" Laura nudged her with her elbow.

Elizabeth slowly forced her eyes open. Sophia's mother was passing a Christmas package to her son under the watchful eye of the guard. The paper was wrinkled, and the bow looked as if it had been used many times before.

With a grimace, Tony ripped open the package. Inside was a black hand-knit sweater. Tony looked at it for a moment, then threw it at his sister. "Here," he muttered. "You wear the ugly thing. What am I going to do with it?"

Tears spilled down his mother's cheeks. She buried her head in her hands and sobbed softly.

"I told you he wasn't worth it, Mama," Sophia said bitterly, staring at her brother through narrowed eyes.

"Stop this, Laura!" Elizabeth cried. "This isn't the real Sophia. This isn't what Tony is like. I don't want to see any more."

"You might as well get used to it, Liz." Laura crossed her arms over her chest. "This is just one stop on the route."

"Time's up," the guard called.

Sophia's mother reached across the table and touched her son's hand with trembling fingers. Tony started to jerk his hand away.

"No, Tony, please," Sophia begged softly. "For Mama, Tony. It's Christmas Eve."

Tony's lower lip trembled. Without meeting his mother's eyes, he squeezed her hand for a brief moment. "I'm sorry, Mama," he whispered. Then he shoved back his chair and followed the guard out the door, never looking back.

"Poor guy," Laura said, sniffling. "You still got that Kleenex, Liz?"

Elizabeth spun to face her. "What are you crying about? You don't even know these people! These are *my* friends, Laura—"

"Sorry. You're absolutely right. I'm not supposed to get emotionally involved. Rule number twenty-three in the handbook." She sniffled again. "But I kind of have a soft spot in my heart for juvenile delinquents."

"This is your fault!" Elizabeth exploded. "You're making me see these things! And they aren't true. They couldn't possibly be true!"

"Don't get angry at me," Laura said defensively. "I just granted you your wish, Liz." Suddenly her eyes went wide. "Wait a second. I know what gives. You're in the Mad-As-Heck phase. Just like my psychology instructor said. Man, I thought old Sigmund was full of it, but I have to admit, so far you're a textbook case."

"Time to go, Mrs. Rizzo," the guard called again.

"Why is he calling her Mrs. Rizzo?" Elizabeth demanded. "She's Mrs. Thomas now. She and Sarah Thomas's father got married. They just got back from their honeymoon in Hawaii."

"Wrong again. Not without you, they didn't."

Elizabeth felt as if the floor beneath her were giving way. "No," she cried, "that's not how it is . . ." Her voice trailed off as she watched Sophia and her mother slowly get to their feet. Their faces were stained with tears. Sophia glared at the guard as he held open the door for them.

"See ya next week," he said with a hint of a smirk. "Although I can't imagine why you bother for that cheap punk."

Sophia spun around, her fists clenched, her eyes filled with rage.

"Please, Sophia," her mother whispered. "Not today. No more fighting today."

Reluctantly Sophia followed her mother out the door without another word, her head hung low.

"Watch this," Laura whispered to Elizabeth. She sauntered up to the guard until she was only inches from his large belly. With a flick of her wrist, she popped open two of the man's shirt buttons. He clutched at his stomach in astonishment.

Elizabeth's head was spinning. *I'm having a nightmare*, she told herself for the hundredth time. *I'll wake up soon, and Laura will be gone and the world will be back to normal. Tony will be back in school and Mr. and Mrs. Thomas will be in love and Sarah and Sophia will be best friends.* She squeezed her eyes shut and pictured Sarah and Sophia laughing together.

"Liz," Laura interrupted. "There's something more you need to know."

Elizabeth's eyes flew open. "I don't want to hear it," she exploded. She brushed past the guard and ran down the cold, dark hallway. "I don't want to know."

"Liz," Laura called. "Listen to me, Liz." Her voice echoed down the empty hall. "Sarah Thomas is dead."

Fourteen

Elizabeth ran out the door into the yard of the reform school. A cold drizzle had begun to fall, and a black blanket of clouds was draped over the city. She ran past the guardhouse and down the gray, dingy street, commanding her legs to go even faster. Her lungs burned. Her eyes stung with tears. Her whole body seemed to ache with a pain she didn't understand, but she knew one thing—she had to get away from Laura.

Sarah Thomas is dead. Elizabeth could still hear Laura's words echoing down the hall. *Sarah Thomas is dead.*

Laura was the reason Sweet Valley had turned into this depressing, dismal world, a place where nothing was what it seemed or what it was supposed to be. A world where Elizabeth had been reduced to a shadow. Laura was the reason she was so unhappy and confused.

Suddenly she remembered Suzannah and Al and the look of pain on Mrs. Glass's face that morning. She remembered Jessica's fury. She remembered going to the mall, her feelings of panic and desperation, of wanting to run away.

Of wishing she'd never been born.

She paused at a street corner, whipping around long enough to see if Laura was following her. So far, so good. She was nowhere in sight. She checked the street sign. Seventeenth and East Main. She'd been here before. So why did everything seem so strange? Everything was where it should be, but in tiny, almost unnoticeable ways, there were differences. Just enough to make everything feel distorted as if she were seeing a reflection in a carnival mirror.

She heard a noise behind her and began to run again. She was going so fast, she didn't even notice the overturned garbage can blocking the sidewalk or the scrawny little dog pawing through its contents. She ran smack into the can with her right shin, but her leg passed through it as if it— or *she*—weren't there.

"There you are!"

Elizabeth's heart leaped into her throat as Laura popped out from behind a hedge, brushing leaves out of her braid. "Laura!" she cried. "How did you—"

"Trade secret. You don't expect me to keep running after you, do you? I'm not cut out for this marathon stuff. Fortunately, this time you ran in the right direction. We're almost there."

"Almost where?"

"To the cemetery. There's something I need to show you."

Elizabeth shivered. "There's nothing I want to see there."

"You asked about Mr. Thomas and Mrs. Rizzo. Don't you want to know why they didn't get married?"

Elizabeth didn't answer.

"I'll take that as a yes. Well, here's the story, and it's not exactly Brady Bunch material, either."

As Laura spoke, she started to walk. In spite of herself, Elizabeth followed her. It was like being drawn to the scene of an accident. As horrible as it was, she couldn't bring herself to look away.

"Remember that night, months and months ago, when Sarah was alone in her house and she fell down the stairs?" Laura asked.

Elizabeth nodded.

"Well, she died, poor kid—"

"That's crazy!" Elizabeth exploded. "Amy and

my dad and I found Sarah after she fell! She was in the hospital for a while with a concussion, but she's fine now. *Fine.*"

"Nice try, Liz," Laura said a little sadly. "I like that version of the story better, too. Too bad it isn't true. Sarah did die that night, and Mr. Thomas's heart was broken. The guy lives in his house like a hermit now. Seems he feels responsible for Sarah's death."

Laura paused to gaze hungrily in the window of a candy shop. "Do you know how long it's been since I've had a nice malted-milk ball? Or a Goober? Or a Raisinette? Twenty-five years without a Goober." She sighed. "Sorry. I know we're supposed to be talking about your problems, but I have a short attention span. That's why I was in the remedial class. That, and my lousy people skills."

"What people skills?" Elizabeth muttered darkly.

"Exactly. I seem to tick people off."

"Laura." Elizabeth grabbed her by the shoulders and squeezed hard. It felt good being able to touch something. "It's time for you to stop lying to me."

"I'm not lying. I really do annoy people." She pried one of Elizabeth's fingers loose.

"I want you to tell me the truth about Sarah!"

"First promise you won't strangle me, Liz. I

mean, I'm already dead, but it would sound so stupid when I make my report later."

Elizabeth loosened her grip slightly. "I was there, Laura. I saw Sarah lying at the bottom of the stairs. My father had to break a window so we could get to her. I climbed in through the hole. We called the paramedics. We went to see her at the hospital later. I'm telling you, Laura, she's all right!"

"See for yourself, Liz." Laura pointed across the street.

Elizabeth followed her gaze. She read the letters chiseled into a marble arch. "Sweet Valley Memorial Gardens."

"If you don't believe me, maybe you'll believe your own eyes. Go in, hang a right, and head for the willow tree."

Elizabeth let go of Laura and dashed across the street. The cemetery was surrounded by a high iron gate. She went through the main entrance and followed Laura's directions, making her way carefully through the rows of white headstones. Bouquets of red flowers and poinsettia plants decorated many of the graves. The headstones glistened in the mist. Above her the wind set the trees whispering.

The words on the gravestones blurred together as she walked. *Beloved Mother. Precious Infant Son. Beautiful Daughter—*

She stopped. Her breath caught in her throat. A small weeping willow swayed before her in the wind. Next to a vase of fresh red roses, a worn, wet teddy bear wearing a rainbow T-shirt sat perched against a gravestone.

Sarah loved rainbows.

Elizabeth gritted her teeth and forced herself to read the inscription on the headstone:

Sarah Lynn Thomas
Beautiful Daughter, Loving Friend
She Will Live Forever In Our Hearts

"No!" Elizabeth moaned, dropping to her knees on the wet grass. "It can't be!"

"I'm sorry, Liz." Laura stood at her side. "You weren't there when she needed you, and now she's gone."

Elizabeth reached for the little bear, but she could touch only air. She began to sob. The drizzle came down harder, as if the whole world were crying with her.

"Liz?" Laura asked as she paced back and forth. "You OK, Liz? I'm fresh out of tissues. You want to blow your nose on my sleeve?"

Elizabeth stumbled to her feet. "I have to get out of this place," she said.

"Gives you the willies, right? Me too, although

technically I should feel right at home. But there's one more minor stop we have to make while we're here."

Elizabeth kept on going, picking her way past the gravestones. Some were imposing, with marble cherubs and elaborate carving. Some were old and neglected and covered with moss. A few, like the one up ahead, were freshly dug and layered with slowly wilting flowers.

"See that brand-new one?" Laura called as Elizabeth neared the bright white headstone. "I hear it was a nice funeral."

"I don't want to hear about funerals."

"Everybody from the middle school came."

Elizabeth paused in midstride. "The middle school?"

"But then," Laura continued, rearranging a bouquet of daisies on the grave, "I guess Denny had a lot of friends, didn't he?"

"Denny?" Elizabeth repeated, praying she'd heard Laura wrong.

"Denny Jacobsen." Laura sniffed a limp white carnation. "He drowned in a surfing accident. A monster wave hit, his surfboard whacked him on the head, and nobody was around to rescue him."

"Stop it, Laura! You know that's not true!" Elizabeth screamed. "*I* rescued Denny!"

Laura shook her head. Her peace-sign earrings dangled back and forth. "Liz, Liz, Liz. I know you like to write fiction, but *really*. Let's get our facts straight. Denny drowned. Mrs. Jacobsen had a nervous breakdown. The whole family was so bummed out, they decided to move from the valley. Too many downer memories and all that."

"You know, Laura, I'm really starting to hate you," Elizabeth cried.

"You're only now *starting* to hate me? Man, we're falling behind schedule. You're supposed to despise me by now. It's one of the phases. Phase four, is it? I'm not sure. To be honest, I didn't do all that well in that class."

Elizabeth looked away. "Denny didn't drown," she said firmly.

"I'll make a deal with you," Laura said, twisting her love beads around her finger. "You check out his gravestone. If you still don't believe me, I'll prove to you I'm telling the truth."

Elizabeth chewed on her lower lip, considering. She felt like Alice in Wonderland after she'd fallen down the rabbit hole. Nothing made any sense, but she had to keep pretending it did.

"All right," she agreed at last. She walked along the edge of the wet, newly dug earth to the small marble stone covered in flowers. Gently she removed a handful, then a few letters were visible. DENN was all she read, but it was enough.

She turned to Laura. Maybe she could call her bluff. Laura had said she could prove it. Well, let her try.

"All right," Elizabeth said. "Prove it."

For a moment Laura just stood there, chewing on her thumbnail. "I was afraid you'd say that," she murmured. She paced back and forth next to the grave. "I'm not really supposed to do this, is the thing. After all, I only have my learner's permit."

"To drive?"

"To do T-2s."

"What's a T-2?" Elizabeth asked wearily.

"Time Travel. It's a very tricky maneuver, especially without a good map. One wrong turn and we could end up hanging with the Flintstones for eternity."

"This is all just some elaborate trick, isn't it?" Elizabeth said accusingly. "I don't know how you did it or why, but it's all just a horrible trick."

"Fine," Laura said in exasperation. "Fine. We'll do it the hard way. I'll prove to you that Denny's dead. But if you end up stuck in a cave with a bone through your nose, don't blame me."

"I promise."

Laura held out her hand. "Hang on tight and fasten your seat belt," she instructed. "And remind me to turn left when we get to last month."

Fifteen

❄

Suddenly everything stopped dead. The blades of grass no longer caught the breeze. The leaves in the trees no longer whispered. The birds fell silent. The crickets were still. It was as if the whole world had stopped breathing.

Then, slowly, haltingly, things began to move again. But something had changed. Elizabeth was sure of it. The breeze now blew the other way. The chirping of the crickets was oddly distorted, like a recording being played backward.

The sky began to darken as if day had turned to night. Elizabeth stared at the clouds. Above her the stars sped along till they were long white lines. The moon seemed to jump back from the western horizon and fly across the sky, heading east.

A moment later the sun rose. But it wasn't coming from the east. It rose from the west and flew through the sky. Instantly the moon followed in its wake. Soon the sun and moon had formed one continuous blazing line across a sky that pulsated bright blue one second, black the next.

"What's happening?" Elizabeth cried.

"T-2," Laura shouted. "We're going backward in time."

Elizabeth looked down, afraid to watch the frantic setting and rising of the sun and moon. But her eyes met an even more horrifying sight. The ground below her feet was shooting past like a conveyer belt going millions of miles an hour. They seemed to be hovering just inches above it. Here and there she could make out brief, ghostly flashes of buildings and trees.

Then she realized what was happening. The trees, the buildings, even whole mountains, were passing right through her, and through Laura too, leaving them untouched.

"Make it stop!" Elizabeth screamed.

"Not yet," Laura said. "We're not *then* yet."

Elizabeth clutched her head and covered her eyes, closing out the insane visions. She felt dizzy. Her knees buckled. She fell forward, half-unconscious.

"Would you like fries with that?"

Slowly, cautiously, Elizabeth opened her eyes to locate the friendly voice. She was lying face-down on cold, damp sand. Her teeth crunched on grains of it. There was sand in her hair. Sand in her pockets. Sand just about everywhere.

She struggled to stand and wiped her eyes. She was near the beach, her favorite part of the Sweet Valley beach, where she liked to take long walks. The wind whipped around her. Sand pelted her bare arms, stinging like hard rain. Dark clouds galloped across the sky. But at least the sun was standing still, and the ground was firm beneath her.

Behind her she heard voices. "Could I have some ketchup, too?"

Elizabeth spun around. It was Amy! Amy and Maria Slater! They were at the little white concessions trailer at the edge of the beach parking lot.

"Amy!" she called. "It's me, Elizabeth!"

Suddenly something hit her in the back, hard. Elizabeth flew through the air, landing on her hands and knees on the sand with a grunt.

"OK, OK, so it wasn't the smoothest landing," Laura said, brushing off her elbows. She gazed around. "But at least you're not carrying a club and wearing stegosaurus-skin jeans."

"We're on the beach," Elizabeth said when she'd found her breath.

"Of course. I'm not a total moron, you know. This is exactly where I wanted us to be." Laura emptied sand out of her sandals.

"I don't ever want to do that again," Elizabeth said shakily.

Laura shrugged. "Hey, it worked out all right, didn't it? More or less? We ended up pretty close to where we were going." She gazed longingly at the trailer where Amy and Maria were eating. "Actually, I was aiming for the exact spot where Denny got into trouble, but I may still have had corn dogs in the back of my mind. In any case, since we're in the neighborhood, one little corn dog couldn't hurt."

"Laura—"

"I could at least go sniff the caramel corn."

Elizabeth felt a sinking, uneasy feeling in her stomach. Something about the dark clouds, the hard wind, the sight of Amy and Maria at the concession stand . . . it gave her a strange feeling. "What day is it, anyway?" she asked.

"This is the day Denny died, Liz. Unfortunately you weren't here to suggest that you and your friends collect shells for your art project. See?"

Elizabeth followed her gaze. Amy and Maria

were heading across the parking lot toward home.

"Come on," Laura said, trudging across the sand. "The corn dog can wait. I promised I'd show you what happened to Denny."

Elizabeth hesitated. Out on the ocean, the wind was whipping the gray waves into a frenzy. They pounded the shore like the insistent throbbing in her head.

"Come on," Laura called from shoreline.

Reluctantly Elizabeth obeyed. She followed Laura silently as the salty spray stung her cheeks and the white foam sucked at her shoes. They walked for a long time, Elizabeth stepping in the footprints Laura left behind before the waves could erase them.

"There," Laura whispered, stopping suddenly. "Out there."

Elizabeth raised her gaze with effort. Far out in the white-capped water, two tiny figures in red and yellow neon wet suits paddled furiously on their surfboards. Every few seconds they disappeared from view, hidden by the huge swells.

"It's Denny," Elizabeth whispered. "And his big brother."

"Sam, isn't that his name?"

Elizabeth nodded, clenching her fists at her sides.

"They shouldn't be out in weather like this," Laura said. She shook her head sadly. "Though I can't say I blame them. Check out the size of those waves! Major surf!"

"This isn't how it happened," Elizabeth said. "I came by with Maria and Amy. I saw it all happen—"

Suddenly her words were lost in the wind. She watched Denny getting pulled away from his brother by the undertow. She saw the huge wave rising behind Denny, an instant mountain of water that sucked him away from his brother. Denny began to paddle furiously as the wave picked up force. Then he scrambled up onto his board, shimmying back and forth to keep his balance.

The wave crested and Denny glanced behind him frantically. Then, arms outstretched, he rode the giant wall of water as it tumbled behind him, roaring like a thunderclap. For a few seconds he stayed ahead of the crest. But the wave was too fast for Denny. It curled around him into a black, living tunnel.

"I can't watch," Elizabeth moaned. It was too terrible to watch twice in one lifetime.

"You came here to watch. You wanted proof, remember?" Laura said.

Then it happened. The tunnel collapsed. The

wave crashed and foamed and returned to the ocean, sucking Denny down with it. His board flew into the air as if the ocean had chewed it up and spit it back out. It twisted in the air like a colorful bird, then sliced back toward the water.

Landing, as Elizabeth knew it would, on Denny's head.

"He's knocked out!" Elizabeth screamed. She watched in horror as another fierce wave broke over Denny, pulling him under the churning black water.

"He's drowning!" she cried. Elizabeth took off down the sand as the seconds ticked away like days. She leaped into the crashing surf, but the waves sailed right through her.

Right through a *possibility* who wasn't really there at all.

"Denny!" she screamed, but even she couldn't hear her voice above the explosions of surf.

She tried to remember how it had been, how she'd struggled through the waves to reach him. How she thrown her arm around his neck and towed him to shore in the crook of her elbow. How afraid she'd been that she wouldn't make it, that they'd both be lost to the treacherous ocean.

Now, she realized, even if she reached him, she wouldn't be able to touch him. She wouldn't be able to help him at all.

She felt a hand on her shoulder. It had to be Laura. Only she could see or touch or hear the *possibility* named Elizabeth Wakefield.

Laura. Her guardian angel.

"He's washing up over there," Laura said grimly, pointing down the beach.

Elizabeth looked and saw them. A hundred yards down the beach, Sam Jacobsen was cradling the limp, white body of his brother in his arms.

Sixteen

"Come on, Liz," Laura said at last. "You've seen enough of this. Let's move on." She reached for Elizabeth's hand.

"I don't want to go," Elizabeth sobbed. "I don't want to see any more. I just want Denny to be OK."

"He can't be OK," Laura said. "Not without you. It's amazing when you start thinking about it, isn't it? How many lives a person touches one way or another?"

"I don't understand why I'm seeing these things."

"You will after a while. Now, come on. It's time for our next stop."

"I'm sick of this," Elizabeth said. "What's the point, anyway? I screwed up my life, and now that I no longer exist, it looks like I'm still screwing up."

"I sympathize, Liz, really I do. But I'm just the guardian angel in this relationship, dig?" She held out her hands, palm up. "I have my orders."

Elizabeth got slowly to her feet and shook her head. "Dig?"

"Don't give me a hard time. *Dig* and *groovy* may sound old-fashioned to you, but just you wait. I hear bell-bottoms are coming back in style."

Elizabeth stared at Laura as if she were seeing her for the very first time. "Where are you from, anyway, Laura?"

"L.A.," Laura answered as she attempted to retie her braid. "The wrong side of the tracks, you might say."

"Did you have—you know—a family and friends and all that?"

"I'm not an alien, Liz. Of course I had a family and friends and all that. Well," she paused, "not all that many friends, actually."

Elizabeth smiled. "Your lousy people skills, right?"

"Something like that. Plus I was pretty busy. Being a troubled youth is a full-time job." Laura leaped to her feet. "Let's go. We've got a party to go to."

Elizabeth forced herself to look past Laura. Denny was being loaded into the back of the ambulance. A small crowd had gathered to watch.

"Maybe he'll still be OK," she whispered. But somehow she knew she he wouldn't.

"I'm sorry, Liz," Laura said. "Denny's not going to be OK. Not ever. Not in this universe." She took Elizabeth's hand. "Now, let's go."

"Laura?" Elizabeth asked as the wind picked up speed. "How did you . . . um, you know—die, if it's not too personal?"

"I don't like the word *die*. I prefer *expire*. It's so much classier. But enough about me. We're supposed to be concentrating on life without you." She squeezed her eyes shut. "No more questions, OK? I really have to stay focused to get this time-travel stuff right."

"We have to do that again?" Elizabeth moaned.

"Just try shutting your eyes and not thinking about it too much, all right? Try to think Christmas Eve. And whatever you do, don't mention food."

This time Elizabeth only peeked occasionally as the world spun back swiftly in the other direction. When they finally stopped, she smelled apples and cinnamon. She heard the sounds of conversation and of pots and pans banging. In the distance she heard children singing carols.

Elizabeth pried open her eyes just in time to see Winston Egbert walk right through her.

Strange, she thought to herself, *I'm almost getting used to things like that.*

"Yow!" Laura yelled. "Oh, man, I think I messed up."

Elizabeth looked and laughed. Laura's right hand was lodged in a huge chocolate cake.

"They must have moved it right at the last minute," Laura complained. "Those last-second adjustments are incredibly difficult to deal with." She pulled her hand out of the cake and began licking off the icing that stuck to her fingers. "Liz," she said happily, "I think we may just have landed in heaven."

"You ought to know." Elizabeth got to her feet carefully, looking around the room. "But it looks like a big kitchen to me."

"Sure, it's the kitchen of the school cafeteria. And it's Christmas Eve again," Laura said proudly. "Right on target. Plus or minus a few inches."

"Don't try to fool me," Elizabeth said. "I know you were aiming for that cake."

"Hey, that was just good luck." Laura peeled a flat sugarcoated object off her elbow. "Hmm," she said. "Is this supposed to be Santa?" She bit off his head and tossed the rest aside. "Very tasty."

"Could you stop munching long enough to tell me why we're here?" Elizabeth demanded.

"It's time for the Christmas party, Liz. Have you forgotten?" Laura did a little shimmy. "We're going to party hearty."

Elizabeth stared blankly at her.

"Haven't you ever seen anybody do the twist before? It was very big in my day. Would you like to see me frug? Or maybe—"

"Oh, no!" came a voice.

Elizabeth and Laura spun around to see Brooke Dennis standing in the kitchen doorway. She stared in horror at the damaged cake.

Just then Lila and Ellen sauntered in. They were wearing tough-looking black leather jackets. *That's strange*, Elizabeth thought. They weren't wearing a speck of purple.

"The cake!" Lila screamed.

"It looks like someone stuck their whole hand into it," Ellen complained. "Either that, or a gopher decided to move in." She bent over just inches from Elizabeth, dipped her own finger in the icing, and tasted it. "Not bad," she said. Her eyes dropped to the floor. "And look at that! They smushed the Little Drummer Boy! They beheaded him!"

"I guess it wasn't Santa after all," Laura said to Elizabeth.

"Shut up, Ellen," Lila snapped, slapping her hard on the shoulder. She turned and glared at Brooke. "You did this, didn't you, Disgusting Dennis?"

"No, I—" Brooke began.

"Of course you did it, you worthless little snot. And pretty soon everybody's going to know about it."

Ellen unwrapped a candy cane she'd found on the floor. "But how will everyone find out, Lila?"

"We're going to go *tell* everyone, Ellen," Lila said, rolling her eyes. "When exactly are you planning to grow a brain, anyway?"

"But Brooke didn't do it!" Elizabeth cried, forgetting that Lila couldn't hear her.

"I'm telling you, I didn't do it!" Brooke cried. She crossed her arms over her chest and stared at Lila through narrowed eyes. "Not that you'd care. You're just blaming me because you don't like me."

"You got that right," Lila sneered. "Come on, Ellen."

Ellen grabbed another candy cane and dashed after Lila like an eager puppy. Brooke leaned against the tile wall and sighed. Her large brown eyes were filled with tears, but her mouth was set in an angry scowl.

"Why are they treating Brooke this way?" Elizabeth asked. "Nobody ever calls her Disgusting Dennis anymore."

"I guess now that we've all started swiping icing, it wouldn't hurt if I—" Laura reached for the cake.

"Laura!" Elizabeth scolded. "Tell me why they're being so mean to Brooke. I mean, the Unicorns have never gone out of their way to be nice, but still—"

Laura shook her head. "They're not Unicorns anymore. They're the Sharks. And if you think about it for a second, you'll know the reason no one's nice to Brooke. No Elizabeth Wakefield, no friends for Brooke. People still think she's snobby and mean."

"But she's not!" Elizabeth cried, watching as Brooke slunk out of the kitchen. "When she first moved here, she was upset because her parents had gotten divorced. Her mom was in Europe and Brooke really missed her. But I found out about that and we had a big surprise party for her and everything turned out OK . . ." Her words faded away.

"Yeah, I know all about that. Too bad it didn't work out that way," Laura said, heading for the door. "You might have made a big difference in Brooke's life." She jerked her head. "Come on. Let's party down. I've been dying to meet all your friends face-to-face. Get it? Dying?"

Elizabeth stared out the door. Even from the

kitchen she could hear Lila and some of her friends teasing Brooke about the cake.

"Come on, Liz. I think I see Mary Giaccio coming in."

"Mary?" Elizabeth asked, rushing over. "You mean Mary *Wallace*." Elizabeth gazed around the auditorium. It wasn't the festive party scene she'd expected. A few red and green streamers hung across the center of the room, but most appeared to have been ripped down from the ceiling. On a small table covered with red tissue paper a few plates of cookies sat untouched. In the middle of the table a little Styrofoam boy stood at attention, a plastic drum awkwardly tacked to his hand. In the background someone was playing the drummer-boy song on a small stereo.

" 'The Little Drummer Boy'? You call this a party?" Laura put her fingers in her mouth and pretended to gag. "Now, back in my day, we knew how to give a party. You get some black lights, a little Hendrix, turn up the volume till they call the cops. I remember one time I sneaked out to go to a Dead concert, and afterward—"

"Laura," Elizabeth interrupted, "why did you say Mary's last name is Giaccio?"

"Because it *is*." Laura rubbed her temples. "Are you *sure* you were an A student?"

Elizabeth watched as Mary stepped into the

room shyly. Her shoulders slumped and her long blond hair hung limply. She looked like a shadow of the old Mary—the fun, happy, sweet Mary that Elizabeth knew so well.

Mary walked to the table and took a cookie, gazing around the room nervously. Behind her, two older people followed. It took Elizabeth a moment to recognize them.

"Those are the Altmans!" she exclaimed. "Mary's old foster parents. I guess they're acting as chaperons, but why them? Where's Mary's real mom? And Tim?"

Elizabeth met Laura's eyes, then looked down at her hands for several moments. "Mary never found her real mom, did she?" she said softly, her heart sinking. "Not without my help . . ."

"By George, I think she's got it!" Laura exclaimed. "Now I'm going to go try to groove on this pathetic excuse for a party. Will you be OK without me for a few minutes?"

Elizabeth didn't answer. She was staring at poor Mary.

In her mind she could still see that wonderful moment when Mary had finally been reunited with her mother after years of separation.

"Liz." Laura nudged her. "Go mingle."

Elizabeth glanced around the room again. Unfamiliar cliques had formed in the corners while other people wandered around aimlessly. No one seemed to be having a very good time. "Mingle?" she said. "Look at these people, Laura. Everyone looks so miserable."

"Still, there's a guy over there I kind of have my eye on. See the one playing with the—what do you call that? A video game?"

"That's Todd!" Elizabeth exclaimed.

"Very cute."

"He's *my* boyfriend, Laura! Well, sort of."

"Not anymore, he isn't."

"You can't go hit on him."

Laura smiled tolerantly. "I wouldn't worry too much, Liz. Unless he's got a thing for invisible dead chicks, I'm not much of a threat."

Elizabeth studied Todd's face. "Even he looks different," she said sadly. "He always has a smile on his face. I mean, he's the nicest guy in the world. And look at him over there playing video games by himself, ignoring everyone." She sighed. "I wish I could talk to him just for a minute."

"Sorry. I'm fresh out of wishes."

"It wouldn't matter anyway. These aren't my friends anymore. Everybody's changed." Elizabeth pointed across the room. "Look at the Morrises over there. See how the kids are all moping? They look like someone died."

"Well, in a way, someone did."

Elizabeth grabbed Laura's arm. "Don't tell me—"

"No, Patrick's not dead. He ran away a while back, though."

"Where? Where is he?"

Laura averted her eyes. "Who knows, with runaways?" she said curtly. "He needed help, and no one was there to give it to him." She cleared her throat. "It happens."

"But—"

"He's gone, Liz. Figure it out."

The sudden anger in Laura's voice took Elizabeth by surprise. "I didn't mean to upset you," she apologized.

"Forget it. I was just feeling sorry for the kid, that's all." She shrugged. "Not that it matters anymore." Without another word, she stalked off toward the refreshment table.

"Laura?" Elizabeth called. She'd gotten so used to having Laura nearby that she suddenly felt desperately alone without her. "Laura?" she called again, louder. "Can you at least tell me if my sister's coming to the party?"

Laura turned around. Her face was grim. "You ask too many questions, Liz," she said, and then she disappeared into the crowd.

Seventeen

"Mingle," Elizabeth repeated under her breath as she watched Laura head into the crowd. "If Laura wants me to mingle, fine, I'll mingle."

She made her way through the room, slowly circulating. She tried to step out of people's way, but sometimes she couldn't and they would simply walk through her. She felt like a little child at an adult party. No matter how she tried, no one would pay the slightest bit of attention to her. *I might as well be invisible,* she thought, and then she remembered that she *was* invisible. In fact, she wasn't really there at all.

It's like walking through a dream with my eyes open, Elizabeth realized as she watched scene after scene unfold.

No. It was like walking through a nightmare.

*   *   *

Amy, Maria, and Billy huddled together in a corner. From time to time, one of them would giggle nervously. When Ken Matthews walked by, Amy cast him a shy smile, but he ignored her.

"Look what I brought," Maria said. "It's the new *Sixers*, hot off the presses." She reached into her purse and pulled out the newspaper, several sheets of copier paper stapled together at one corner.

"Read Lila's gossip column," Amy urged excitedly. "Who knows? Maybe she mentioned one of us."

"You wish," Billy said with a sigh.

"Here it is," Maria said. She cleared her throat. " '*Shark Bites*, by Lila Fowler,' " she read. " 'Guess whose daddy just got back from the Big Apple with a very special gift for a certain very special daughter? Next time you see yours truly in the hall, check out the diamond bracelet on her wrist—IF YOU DARE! But be sure to wear your shades, kids—these babies could blind you!' "

Amy gazed over at Lila. "Wow, Lila's lucky," she said in an awestruck voice. "I'd give anything to be her for a day!"

"I'd settle for an hour!" Billy added.

"Wait!" Maria said excitedly. "Amy! I think there's something in here about you!"

Amy's eyes opened wide. "Let me see that," she said, grabbing the newspaper. She scanned the page hopefully. "Here," she said. "Here it is. 'BELIEVE IT OR NOT . . . My very reliable sources inform me that two—count 'em, two—boys are actually planning to try out for the prestigious Boosters cheerleading squad. (As if they'd have a prayer!) Their names? You heard it here first, gang! Bachelor number one: Winston Egbert, nerd of the century. And number two: Amy Sutton! (Whoops! Sources inform me that Amy Sutton is actually just a *tom*boy. Oh, well. Either way, she'll never be a Booster!)' "

Amy's cheeks blazed as her eyes began to glisten with tears. She threw the paper onto the floor.

"That's OK, Amy," Maria said. "You wouldn't really want to be a Booster. Think of all the practicing and work."

Janet Howell sauntered past. She looked at Amy, then at the newspaper on the floor. "Oh, well, Amy," she said, sneering. "Maybe you can try out next year." She turned to leave, then spun back around. "And in the future, treat Lila's column with a little more respect, got it?"

Amy stared straight ahead, fighting back her tears.

"I said, got it?"

"We've got it, Janet," Billy said quickly,

rushing to pick up the newspaper.

"Great party, don't you think, Janet?" Maria added nervously.

Janet laughed. "How would *you* know?"

They watched in silence as Janet walked away, still laughing to herself. Amy wiped away a tear impatiently with the back of her hand. "Come on," she said. "Let's go try some of those cookies."

Winston Egbert stood near the refreshment table, pouring himself a glass of punch.

"Stay away from those cookies," Ken warned. "I think they may be fossilized."

"Like my grandmother's fruitcake," Winston said, laughing. "Every year she drags it out, and every year no one eats it. I swear it's older than she—"

"Well, if it isn't the Egg-man."

Charlie Cashman and Jerry McAllister swaggered up to the table.

"Try some cookies," Winston said evenly, sipping his punch. "They're delicious."

"Maybe I'll just have some punch instead." Charlie reached past Winston for the punch-bowl ladle. Suddenly he jerked his arm back and elbowed Winston in the stomach. Winston doubled over, his punch glass flying. It landed at Todd's feet, splashing his sneakers with red liquid.

"What'd you do that for, Charlie?" Ken said.

Charlie shrugged. "Bored, I guess." He turned to Jerry. "You know what, Jerry? I'm feeling hungry all of sudden. Think maybe I'll scramble me up an egg." He poked Winston in the chest with his index finger. "Get it, Egg-man?"

Winston gulped. "Very witty. Have you ever considered stand-up comedy?"

"I like fall-down comedy, myself," Charlie sneered. He thrust against Winston's shoulders with both hands and sent him flying through the air. Winston landed with a grunt.

Several people turned to stare, but no one said a word. "Cut it out, Charlie," Ken finally said, but Jerry pinned his arm behind his back.

"Todd?" Winston turned to his friend hopefully. "Could you help me out here?"

Todd wiped punch off one of his sneakers. "Give it up, Winston," he muttered, turning back to his video game.

"Come on, Todd," Winston said. "Three against two, we might not get totally beaten to a pulp."

"Not my fight," Todd said, turning away.

Winston watched, his face crumpled in disappointment, as Todd walked sullenly away.

"Get up, Egg-man," Charlie jeered.

"Come on, boys. Enough." Mary's foster dad,

Mr. Altman, walked over, hands on his hips. "This is a Christmas party, or have you forgotten? Settle this another time."

"I'll finish you up later," Charlie said to Winston. He gave him an icy smile. "Merry Christmas, Egg-man."

Jerry released Ken while Winston got to his feet unsteadily.

Winston looked over at Todd, who was leaning against the exit door, watching the evening sky unfold.

"You know," Winston said, "sometimes I really hate the holidays."

Outside on the front lawn, the Sharks had gathered behind a small stand of pine trees. The sky was turning from velvety blue to black. A few pale stars were blinking in the darkness.

Elizabeth gasped as she saw Tamara Chase light up a cigarette. What had happened to these girls? Sure, the Unicorns could be selfish and snobby, but they were nothing like this.

Tamara's face glowed briefly in the flickering match light. "Anyone see the parent patrol?" she asked.

"It's cool," Lila said. She reached for the cigarette and inhaled slowly. "The only person who saw us come out here was Todd, and he's too much of a wimp to narc."

"So what's the plan?" Kimberly asked.

"Shut up and I'll tell you. It's brilliant, if I do say so myself," Janet said proudly.

"Of course it's brilliant," Ellen said, "if you came up with it, Janet."

Janet scowled. "Stop sucking up to me, Ellen."

"Sorry," Ellen whimpered. "I thought it was my duty as a Shark to suck up."

"Your duty as a Shark is to keep your mouth shut," Lila scolded. "Now, tell everyone the plan, Janet."

Janet grabbed Lila's cigarette. "Here's the deal. We go to Jessica Wakefield's house tonight—"

Elizabeth froze at the mention of the name.

"Why Jessica?" Ellen asked.

"Don't go all philosophical on us, Ellen. Your brain's under enough strain." Janet shook her cigarette at Ellen for effect. "We're going to Jessica's because we like to pick on her, all right?"

Elizabeth immediately felt worried for her sister but also relieved that Jessica wasn't part of this group. Where *was* Jessica tonight? It was so strange that she wasn't here. Her twin was always the center of every party.

"And then what?" Tamara asked.

"Tell them the good part," Lila urged.

Janet paused for dramatic effect. "We go to Jessica's house, and we tell her we're going to let her join as an associate Shark—"

"What's that?" Ellen interrupted.

"An associate Shark," Lila said, glaring, "is a member who can't vote. It's like a Shark with no teeth, which is what you're going to be real soon if you don't shut up."

"*Anyway*," Janet continued, "we tell Jessica that first she has to do some dare, something really impossible. Then—" she flicked her ashes onto Ellen's shoes, "we sit back and watch the fun."

"But what's the dare going to be?" Tamara asked.

"That's why we're having this meeting," Janet said. "I was going to decide myself, but then I thought, hey, why should I have all the fun? I mean, it *is* Christmas. So in the spirit of the holidays, I thought we'd vote on how to make Jessica suffer. You know—democracy in action."

"You're a saint, Janet," Ellen said.

Janet shot her a warning look. Ellen winced.

"Did that count as sucking up?" she asked nervously.

Kimberly leaned against a tree, lost in thought. "How about we dare her to steal something?"

"Too easy," Janet declared. "I was hoping for something a little more . . . you know—*dramatic*."

"We could ask her to jump off a cliff," Tamara said.

Janet shook her head. "That's dramatic, Tamara, but it would probably be better if she didn't *die*. Who knows what might happen if they connected us to it?"

"Major detentions," Lila said ominously.

"Probably," Janet agreed. "Although that would be good for our image." She tapped her foot on the ground impatiently. "Still, a little danger couldn't hurt."

"I remember a slumber party when we were little," Ellen said. "We were playing truth or dare, and Kimberly dared me to kiss Randy Mason on the lips the next day at school."

Lila rolled her eyes. "Is there a point to this story, Ellen?"

"Well, Janet said to come up with something dangerous, and I can't think of anything more dangerous than actual lip contact with that pimple factory."

"I can see I'm going to have to do the thinking for all of us," Janet said with a heavy sigh. "As usual." She tossed her cigarette to the grass and ground it with her shoe. "I'll come up with something on the way. Come on, Sharks. This party's worthless anyway. Let's go give Jessica our little Christmas present."

Elizabeth ran back into the party as fast as her legs could carry her. The nightmare was getting worse. Jessica was in trouble, and Elizabeth had to find her before it was too late.

Laura was watching two little boys play a video game. She had several cookies in each hand.

"Laura, you've got to help me!" Elizabeth cried. "The Sharks are planning to play some horrible trick on Jessica, and I've got to warn her."

"Man, these video things are cool," Laura said, taking a bite of a chocolate-chip cookie. "I'll bet I could whip you at a game. I mean, you know, if you could play."

"Are you listening to me?" Elizabeth shouted. She grabbed Laura by the shoulders. "My twin is in trouble. I have to find her."

Laura frowned. "I'm not sure you're ready for that, Liz."

"Ready? What are you talking about? I'll go find her myself if I have to."

"No, no, don't go running off again." Laura stuffed a couple cookies in her pockets. "You'll need me with you for this. And anyway, this

party is a royal bummer. I mean, they keep playing that drummer-boy ditty. Is that like a big hit
or something? Why not a little Stones, or maybe
some Beatles?"

"Come *on*." Elizabeth yanked Laura toward
the door. "We've got to hurry."

Laura sighed. "Actually, Liz, there's not much
point in hurrying. There's nothing we can do."
But Elizabeth was already running out the door
into the chill night air.

Eighteen

❄

Elizabeth turned another corner. If she crossed through town, she could get to her house before the Sharks. Maybe she could somehow get through to Jessica. She didn't know how, but there had to be a way.

Grove Street was straight ahead, a crowded street lined with dilapidated buildings and a few tired-looking bars. She could take Grove over to Main, and if she cut through that parking lot—

"Liz." Laura yanked her to a stop. "I'm dying here."

"Very funny, Laura."

"No, I mean it. I can't breathe. I can't run this fast. Please, can't we fly?"

"We'll end up at a Baskin-Robbins. I know you. You've got a one-track mind."

Laura yanked harder. "I'm not sure you want to go through with this, Liz."

"You've shown me everyone else. Why not my own family?" Elizabeth demanded. She took off again, past another seedy bar.

"Liz!" Laura cried. "Not that way!"

Suddenly Elizabeth froze. There was someone in the bar she'd just passed. Someone familiar.

She took a few steps back. A string of Christmas lights had been tacked along the edge of the window. Half of them were burned out. Elizabeth put her nose to the glass. The man inside was hunched over the bar, clutching a small glass. She couldn't quite make out his face, but she recognized the worn brown overcoat.

"Wait, Liz!" Laura called, but it was too late.

Elizabeth walked through the door into the bar. Aside from the man at the counter, there were only three other customers, a group of older guys sitting in a booth. The little room was dark and smelled stale and tired. An old jukebox in a corner was playing "Jingle Bell Rock."

Elizabeth took a step closer to the man. She remembered that coat. She remembered the wide belt and its smooth collar. She remembered tugging on the sleeve when she was little. She remembered the smell of fresh air it had carried when her father had come home from work and she and Jessica had run to greet him. "Dad?" she whispered.

He shoved his glass down the bar. "One more, Doug," he said.

"OK, Ned. One more for the road," the bartender said. "But that's it. We're closing up soon, buddy."

Elizabeth stood directly beside her father. His face was pale and thin. A dark stubble of beard covered his chin. His eyes had a haunted, empty look.

"You got plans for Christmas Eve, Ned?" the bartender asked as he refilled his glass.

"Plans?" Mr. Wakefield gave a short, hollow laugh. "Yeah, big plans, Doug. Me and the kids and the wife. A big, warm family get-together."

The bartender stared at Mr. Wakefield. Elizabeth thought she saw pity in his eyes. "Holidays can be tough," he said at last.

Mr. Wakefield took a long swallow of his drink. "Every day is tough," he said, twisting his mouth into a smile as his eyes grew moist.

But it wasn't his eyes or his bitter smile that Elizabeth was staring at in horror.

It was the fourth finger of his left hand, where his wedding ring used to be.

"I'm sorry, Liz," Laura said as Elizabeth ran

from the bar, sobbing uncontrollably. "I tried to warn you."

"I'm going home," Elizabeth managed through her tears. "And don't try to stop me."

With Laura by her side she ran for what seemed like forever, past dark storefronts and empty parking lots, past stray dogs and lonely street people huddled in the darkness. She ran and ran and ran until she couldn't feel her legs anymore. *Home,* she told herself. *I have to go home.*

Up ahead she saw the homeless shelter. For a moment she paused, gasping for air. *I don't have time to look,* she muttered. *I have to go home.*

But something drew her to the window of the little building. Almost against her will she peeked inside. There they were just as she'd been afraid they would be.

Suzannah, Al, and Mrs. Glass sat huddled on a cot in one corner, listening to a small choir of children sing off-key carols. Suzannah and Al were each holding a small bag of candy. Elizabeth knew they were the only gifts the staff at the shelter could manage on its meager budget.

She dropped her eyes. She didn't want to see any more.

"Too bad," Laura said. "Without your help . . ."

"Don't tell me," Elizabeth warned angrily. "With or without my help, it wouldn't have made a difference. I tried to help the Glasses and I made things worse for them, remember?"

"Maybe so," Laura said. "We'll never know now, will we?"

Elizabeth didn't wait to hear any more. She began to run again, even faster now. At last she reached her own neighborhood. Yellow light spilled through the windows of familiar houses. She knew them all. Amy's house. Janet's house. The old ramshackle Spanish mansion next door to Janet's, where Nora Mercandy lived with her grandparents. And, of course, there was Lila's estate—as always, encrusted with tiny, twinkling white lights, more lights than anywhere else in town.

"Man, aren't we there yet?" Laura gasped.

"Almost," Elizabeth said, feeling a sudden, inexplicable burst of hope.

But when they got to her street, for some strange reason, her house was nowhere to be seen. Elizabeth ran to the end of the street, her puzzlement slowly turning to panic. "I don't understand," she said, checking a street sign. "I know this is the right street."

"There." Laura dropped onto the curb and pointed. "Over there."

Elizabeth shook her head. "No, that's not my house. Look at it. It's a mess."

"Look again, Liz."

Elizabeth felt something inside her go taut like a rubber band about to break. She stepped onto the lawn. It was overgrown with weeds. The paint on the house was peeling. One shutter hung at an odd angle. An upstairs window—*her* bedroom window—was broken. There wasn't a single twinkling light, not a bit of Christmas greenery, anywhere in sight.

But there was an address on the mailbox. 1214 CALICO DRIVE.

"This can't be my house," she whispered even though she knew it was.

She walked up to the front porch. Her whole body trembled as she stood at the door, dreading what she would see when she stepped inside.

Ninteen

It was all the same and yet all so different.

It wasn't the dirty clothes or the dust or the trash lying strewn about that bothered Elizabeth so much. For some reason what broke her heart was the pathetic, spindly Christmas tree in the corner. It was barely decorated, with just a few strands of tinsel and an ornament or two that Jessica had made when she was little. A handful of presents sat scattered beneath it.

Elizabeth walked over to the fireplace. Three stockings hung from the mantel. "Mom," Elizabeth read. "Steven. Jessica."

She heard water running in the kitchen. When she got there she found her mother leaning against the sink, gazing out into the black night. Elizabeth gasped when she saw her face. Her mother looked tired and haggard and so much older.

"Mom?" she whispered. She ached to hug her close.

Mrs. Wakefield sighed heavily.

"Tell me what's wrong, Mom," Elizabeth begged. "Why am I seeing these awful things? Why are you so unhappy?"

There was another sigh, only this time it came from the refrigerator. Laura was gazing inside, scanning the contents.

"Nothing here but some moldy bologna," she reported. She jumped onto a countertop. "I can tell you what happened to your family," she said. "If you're sure you want to hear it."

"Tell me," Elizabeth pleaded, her voice trembling. "Why is my mom so sad? Why isn't my dad here, too?"

"Your parents are divorced, Elizabeth," Laura said gently.

"But they would never get divorced! Never! They love each other!"

"Sometimes love isn't enough, Liz. A while back rumors started circulating about your mom having an affair—"

"I remember that. It was all a big mistake," Elizabeth interrupted. "My mom was really busy with her job. She'd been seeing this man, a client of hers, a lot, and well, one thing led to another and we jumped to conclusions—"

"It turned out differently without you there. Jessica really believed your mother was in love with another man. When your father heard about it, he was crushed. Your mom and dad couldn't trust each other anymore. Without you to get to the bottom of things, their marriage grew more and more rocky."

"No," Elizabeth sobbed. She stood by her mother's side, yearning for her touch. She wanted to be held like a little child, to hear her mother say that everything would turn out all right. But no one could hold her now.

"After your parents split up," Laura continued as she searched through a cupboard for food, "there was a terrible custody battle. A real mess. They both nearly went bankrupt with lawyers' fees, fighting each other. Which," she added ruefully, "I guess explains why there isn't a single good munchie in this pantry. Haven't you guys ever heard of Cheese Doodles?"

"I'm outta here," someone called.

Elizabeth gasped. It sounded like Steven's voice.

Mrs. Wakefield ran out of the kitchen to the front door. Elizabeth and Laura followed close behind.

Steven was slouched against the doorjamb, his arms crossed over his chest. At least, Elizabeth *thought* it was Steven. The sullen-faced boy was wearing a ripped black T-shirt, faded jeans, and black boots. His shoulder-length hair was tied back in a loose ponytail, and dark strands of hair hung in his eyes. In one earlobe a diamond earring glittered. On his right arm, half-hidden by his T-shirt, were the ugly red and blue marks of a new tattoo.

"Don't go, Steven," Mrs. Wakefield pleaded. She reached for his arm, but he shook her off angrily.

"Watch the artwork," he warned. "It cost me a fortune."

"Steven." Mrs. Wakefield rubbed her eyes wearily. "It's Christmas Eve. Can't we all just have one nice family evening together?"

"What family?" Steven scoffed. He jerked his head at the three stockings on the mantel. "Looks to me like ol' Ned's missing in action."

Mrs. Wakefield's expression hardened. "I don't want you going out tonight, Steven. Not with those hoods you call friends."

"They're not hoods. They're just misunderstood youths." Steven smirked at his mother. "We have a lot in common, actually. We all come from dysfunctional families."

"Two of those *friends* were arrested last week," Mrs. Wakefield reminded him, her voice icy.

"Those charges are bogus." Steven pushed open the screen door. "You wait. The cops'll drop them."

"Do I have to remind you you're still on probation, young man? One wrong move, and you could be back in juvenile court again." Mrs. Wakefield wrung her hands. "I know you're up to something, Steven. I can feel it."

"Chill, Alice. It's cool." Steven gave her a menacing grin. "We're just going to help Santa deliver presents." Without another word, he shot through the door and leaped off the porch.

Mrs. Wakefield ran out the door after him. "Will you at least be home to open gifts tomorrow morning?" she called desperately.

Steven stopped in midstride halfway across the lawn. "Did you get me that CD player I want?"

"Steven, you know we don't have that kind of money—"

"Then the answer's no."

Mrs. Wakefield turned slowly and came back into the house. She walked through the dark living room and plugged in the lights on the little Christmas tree. Carefully she wound up one of the ornaments, a china angel on a tiny music box. Elizabeth knew it well. Mr. Wakefield had bought it for his wife the first Christmas after they were married. That year it had been the only ornament on their tree.

Mrs. Wakefield slumped onto the couch in the dark living room. The little music box tinkled sweetly. *Silent night, holy night . . .*

"Oh, Ned," she whispered, and then she began to cry.

Crying herself, Elizabeth slowly followed Laura up the familiar staircase. When she reached the door to her bedroom, she stood for several minutes, staring at the knob.

"What's wrong?" Laura asked.

"I want to go in, but I can't," Elizabeth whispered. "I'm afraid."

Laura twisted the knob and the door swung open. Inside were stacks of cardboard boxes. An ironing board sat where her bed should have been. The walls were bare. Dust covered the floor like a carpet.

"See?" Laura said. "Just storage."

Elizabeth took a tentative step inside. "But this is my room. My desk should be right over there." She ran her fingers along the bare wall. "And my poster of the Chincoteague ponies should be here."

Laura put her hands on her hips. "I'll admit it could use some redecorating."

Elizabeth gazed out the window at the cold vast sky, brushing the tears from her cheeks. "Laura?" she asked. "How could Steven have changed so much?"

"Your parents' divorce really shook Steven up," Laura replied. "Sometimes hard times make people hard."

Suddenly a loud sob met their ears. "Jess!" Elizabeth whispered. She dashed for the door, but Laura held up a warning finger. "Liz," she said, "Jessica's changed, too, OK?"

"Everyone's changed," Elizabeth said bitterly.

"I just want you to be prepared. Steven got tough, but Jessica . . . well, Jessica turned in on herself. She's not the Jessica you're expecting to see."

Elizabeth pushed past her down the hall. Jessica's door was open. She was lying face-down on her bed, sobbing loudly. Her hair was a mousy dark blond, as if she hadn't been outside in the sunshine in a very long time. But that was the only change Elizabeth could see. She waited, hoping Jessica would move, wanting to get a better look to assure herself that Laura had been wrong. But Jessica just lay there, her head buried in the crook of her arm. Every so often she let out another shuddering sob.

Elizabeth walked around the room. It wasn't

so very different from what she remembered, was it? The bedspread was still pink. There was still a Johnny Buck poster on the wall. She peeked into Jessica's closet. No, it no longer bulged with clothes, but then, that was because Jessica liked to borrow half of Elizabeth's wardrobe. Still, the clothes looked worn and frayed and frequently mended. And the purple accessories—the belts and ribbons and skirts— were nowhere to be seen.

"Man, you guys have lousy taste in the nineties," Laura commented as she glanced over Jessica's jewelry chest. "I mean, no love beads?"

Elizabeth went over to Jessica's desk. There was an English paper on it. *C-*, Elizabeth read. *Please try harder!* She smiled ruefully. At least some things never changed.

She reached for a framed picture. It showed the family in happier days. Mr. and Mrs. Wakefield and Steven were watching Jessica blow out candles on a birthday cake. Elizabeth counted them. Seven. Jessica was smiling into the camera. Her blond hair caught the light and glistened. Her blue-green eyes glowed. Behind her, something rustled. Elizabeth turned. Jessica was getting up, reaching for a tissue to wipe her eyes.

"No!" Elizabeth cried. "That's not Jessica!"

Laura nodded. "She's changed, huh?"

Changed. That wasn't even the word for it. Not like Steven, not like her mother or father. With them, somehow, Elizabeth still sensed a glimmer of their old selves lingering somewhere beneath the despair.

But this Jessica could never have been the Jessica Elizabeth knew and loved. Her short, greasy hair hung limply in her eyes. She wore thick glasses and an ill-fitting plaid jumper. Her skin was sallow, her eyes red from crying.

But it wasn't her looks that made Elizabeth ache. Those were just the surface changes. It was the desperate sadness in those blue-green eyes, a sadness that told Elizabeth Jessica didn't trust or love anyone anymore—not even herself.

"Oh, Jess," Elizabeth whispered. "Please don't be so sad. I know things are tough right now, but they'll get better. I promise they will."

"Why should she believe that?" Laura asked. "*You* didn't."

Downstairs the doorbell rang. "Jessica?" Mrs. Wakefield called after a moment. "There are some friends here to see you."

"What friends?" Jessica called, frowning.

"It's us, Jessica! Lila and Janet and Ellen!"

Jessica's eyes went wide. "I'll—I'll be right down!" she yelled excitedly.

"Don't go, Jess, *please*," Elizabeth pleaded. "*Please* try to hear me somehow."

"She can't hear you, Liz," Laura scolded. "You know better than that."

Jessica went to her dresser mirror. She wiped her nose and ran a comb through her hair. She smiled at her reflection. Dissatisfied, she tried again. "Hi, Janet!" she said brightly, practicing her entrance. "What brings you here?"

"*No,* Jess," Elizabeth groaned. "You don't need them. There will be other friends. *Nice* friends."

Jessica shook her head and sighed. "Oh, well," she said. "Here goes nothing." She started out the door.

"*Please, Jessica!*" Elizabeth cried.

For a brief moment Jessica paused. She turned her head, her eyes narrowed, staring into space. Then she shrugged and dashed off toward the stairs.

"You tried," Laura said consolingly.

Elizabeth shook her head. "Not hard enough."

Twenty

"Jess! Long time no see!" Janet called as Jessica made her way nervously down the stairs.

"Girls, I don't think we've ever met," Mrs. Wakefield said. "I'm Jessica's mother."

Janet shook her hand energetically. "Pleased to meet you, Mrs. Wakefield. I'm Janet Howell, and this is my cousin Lila Fowler."

"Fowler? Oh, of course. You must live in that big estate with all the pretty Christmas lights. It's a lovely house."

"Yes, ma'am," Lila replied sincerely. "We've been very blessed."

"W-why are you guys here?" Jessica asked shyly, still cowering at the foot of the stairs.

"We thought you might like to join us, Jessica," Janet said. "We're going caroling, and we could use a nice voice like yours."

"B-but I can barely sing at all," Jessica said.

"You're too modest, Jess!" Lila exclaimed. "Isn't she, Ellen?"

Ellen frowned. "I don't know. I've never even heard her—"

"It would just be for an hour or so," Janet interrupted. "You could spare her for a little while, couldn't you, Mrs. Wakefield?"

Mrs. Wakefield craned her neck to see out the door. The rest of the Sharks were gathered at the curb. Charlie and Jerry had joined them.

"Are those the rest of your carolers?" Mrs. Wakefield asked.

"Yes, ma'am," Janet replied. "We could use a few more low voices, as you can see, but Ellen helps out with the bass parts."

"I didn't hear you singing," Mrs. Wakefield said doubtfully.

"Sure we were singing," Ellen said. "We just finished, uh, 'Good King What's-his-name.' Over at your neighbor's house."

"Jessica, it's getting late," Mrs. Wakefield said. "I really don't think this is a good idea."

"Please, Mom," Jessica pleaded. "I'll be back in an hour. I promise."

"An hour should give us plenty of time," Janet said.

Say no, Elizabeth begged from her perch on the stairs. *Please don't let her go, Mom.*

Mrs. Wakefield sighed. "An hour, then, but that's it. I don't want to have to spend Christmas Eve alone."

"Goodness, no," Janet exclaimed. "We'll have her home safe and sound before you know it."

"Take your jacket, honey," Mrs. Wakefield reminded Jessica.

"Good idea," Lila said sweetly. "It is a little nippy out this evening."

Jessica retrieved her jacket from the hall closet. "I'm all set," she said excitedly.

"Have fun," Mrs. Wakefield called as Jessica filed out with the Sharks. "And be careful."

Elizabeth grabbed Laura's arm. "We have to follow her," she said.

"What's the point, Liz? It's not like you can make any difference."

"She's my twin," Elizabeth said firmly.

"Not anymore, she isn't. You were never born, remember?"

"I have to know if she's going to be OK."

"If you insist." Laura started down the steps. "Just don't say I didn't warn you, all right?"

At the door, Elizabeth paused. Mrs. Wakefield was staring out the living room window. Her gaze was as faraway as the stars. "I love you, Mom," Elizabeth whispered.

Mrs. Wakefield closed her eyes and sighed almost as if she'd heard.

"Hey, guys," Lila called to the group assembled in the street, "look who's joining us."

"Jessica!" Kimberly said. "Aren't we lucky?"

Charlie made a kissing noise. "Jessica, baby," he said. "Looking good!"

Jessica grinned. "Hi, everybody. So where do we go to carol?"

"Carol?" Tamara asked, nearly choking.

Janet put her arm around Jessica and led her down the street. The others fell into step beside them. "We're not really going caroling, Jess," she said. She winked. "But then, you knew that, didn't you?"

"I—well, *sure*," Jessica said.

"That was just a cover story to shut your mom up," Lila said.

Jessica laughed nervously. "I knew that."

"You want a cigarette, Jess?" Janet asked, reaching into the pocket of her leather jacket.

"Oh, no," Jessica said quickly. "I don't smoke."

"Of course you don't," Janet said with a smirk. "It's a nasty habit."

Ellen leaned close to Janet. "When are you

going to tell her?" she asked in a loud whisper.

"When I'm good and ready," Janet snapped.

Jessica cast Janet a nervous glance. She stopped walking and gazed back at her house, chewing on her lower lip. "I think maybe I should be heading on back," she said. "My mom's all by herself, and it is Christmas Eve. I don't exactly feel right about leaving her, and since we're not going caroling—"

"Isn't she just the most thoughtful girl?" Janet interrupted. "That's why we like you, Jessica. Isn't it, guys?"

There was a low murmur of agreement.

"So I guess I'll just—" Jessica began.

"Come on," Janet urged. "We're going to Lila's for a little party. Wouldn't you like to see the Fowler mansion from the inside?"

Jessica's eyes went wide. "Well, sure. I guess."

"I don't let just anybody in my house," Lila pointed out. "This is a rare opportunity."

"I don't know. . . ."

"Stop worrying about your mom," Janet soothed. "Do we look like we're worried about our moms?"

"This is your chance to get to know us a little," Kimberly pointed out.

"You're not afraid of us, are you, Jessica?" Janet asked.

"No." Jessica managed a tiny laugh. "Well, maybe a little. I mean, you're the Sharks. Everybody's a little afraid of you."

Lila slapped her on the back. "We're just regular people," she said. "Just regular people, only cooler."

"This is the opportunity of a lifetime," Tamara said. "We're giving you the chance to be in the company of coolness."

Jessica took a deep breath. "OK," she said, forcing a smile.

"You won't regret it," Janet promised. "This will be a night to remember."

As Jessica and the Sharks turned down the street that led to the Fowler estate, Elizabeth and Laura kept pace alongside them.

"Why is she going with them?" Elizabeth asked.

"I suppose she wants to feel like she belongs," Laura said, shrugging. "Or maybe she just likes their jackets. *I* do."

Elizabeth clenched her fists. Every time she looked at Jessica she felt pity and sadness and rage. "Doesn't she understand there are lots of other people she could be friends with? Nice people like Billy or Maria or Amy."

"Somewhere back in time Jessica lost her way," Laura said. "She doesn't know what she wants anymore. She needs someone to help her through the rough spots. Don't we all?" She laughed, but there was a hint of bitterness in her voice.

They watched as the Sharks led Jessica up the long, sweeping entranceway to Lila's home. Little white lights blanketed the trees and hedges like snow. A huge evergreen wreath tied with a red bow graced the front door.

"Here it is," Lila said to Jessica. "Home sweet home. Be sure to wipe your feet. Our house-keeper's a real witch."

"It's so . . . huge," Jessica said. "I've never seen such a big house."

"You ain't seen nothing yet," Janet promised.

Laura nudged Elizabeth. "Shall we?"

"I can't stand this," Elizabeth muttered. "Why do they have to tease her this way? Why can't they just get on with whatever they have planned?"

"It's like cats with a mouse," Laura said as she watched the Sharks head inside. "They like to see it suffer first." She started up the walk. "Come on. You said you wanted to watch."

Twenty-one

❄

"This house is incredible," Jessica said as she followed the Sharks upstairs. She paused to gape at the crystal chandelier hanging in the entranceway.

"Check out Lila's bedroom," Kimberly said. "It's totally awesome."

The Sharks made themselves comfortable in Lila's room. Charlie and Jerry cranked up her CD player. Kimberly and Tamara spread out on her bed. Ellen dropped into a chair and began leafing through a magazine.

"So," Janet said, draping her arm around Jessica's shoulders, "what do you think of Lila's place?"

"It's amazing," Jessica said sincerely. She turned to Lila, who was browsing through the dozens of outfits in her walk-in closet. "Your bedroom's practically as big as the whole down-stairs of our house, Lila!"

"What?" Lila glanced over her shoulder. "Oh, yeah, big. I guess it'll do."

"Do?" Jessica cried. "You live like a princess!"

"That's me, Princess Li."

Ellen yawned. "Can we get on with this?" she complained. "I'm bored."

"And I'm hungry," Jerry muttered. "You got anything to eat around here?"

"Why don't you guys go downstairs and raid the kitchen?" Lila suggested. "We're going to have ourselves a little makeover session."

"You mean, like, with makeup?" Jerry demanded.

"We're going to makeover Jessica," Lila announced. "A totally new Jessica Wakefield!"

Charlie laughed. "Good luck."

"We're outta here," Jerry announced. "Let us know when the fun part starts."

Jessica frowned. "Makeover? What do you mean?" She watched the two boys leave, snickering under their breath.

"Sit down, Jessica," Janet said. "I guess it's time to tell you why we brought you here."

"All right!" Ellen tossed her magazine aside.

Jessica sat down nervously on the edge of Lila's bed.

"As you know," Janet began, "the Sharks are the most exclusive organization in Sweet Valley."

Ellen laughed. "Organization?"

"That's right, Ellen, *organization*." Janet cast her a warning look. She paced back and forth in front of Jessica, her arms clasped behind her back. "And, like any exclusive organization, we occasionally decide to recruit new members. We call them associate Sharks."

"They don't have teeth," Ellen offered.

Lila scowled. "Shut up, Ellen."

"I don't understand what this has to do with me," Jessica said meekly.

"We're prepared to offer you a chance to join our organization, Jessica," Janet announced.

Jessica's mouth dropped open. "Me? Why would you want someone like me?"

"I *told* you she'd ask that," Lila hissed.

"It's a fair question," Janet said. She paused to light up a cigarette. "The truth is, Jessica, we need some fresh blood. You know. New ideas. Innovative thinking."

Jessica narrowed her eyes. "But why me?" She made a wry face. "I mean, let's face it. I've never exactly been Ms. Popular."

"We think you could be," Janet said. "With a little work."

"A lot of work," Ellen added.

"Shut up, Ellen," Janet said. She sat down next to Jessica. "That's why we're doing the make-over. If you're going to be a Shark, you have to look the part."

Jessica glanced at her reflection in Lila's full-length mirror. "I don't think I ever could," she said, combing her fingers through her lank hair. "You all look so . . . well, tough."

"What do you mean, tough?" Lila demanded.

"You know. You wear lots of makeup. You've always got those black leather jackets on. Some of you even smoke. And the ones who don't smoke, pop their gum really loudly."

"We're making a fashion statement," Lila said. "You got a problem with that?"

"No," Jessica said quickly. She gazed nervously at Janet.

"Don't worry, Jessica," Kimberly said. "You don't have to do any of that, not yet. After all, you're just going to be an Associate Shark."

Jessica sighed. "I'm not sure . . ."

"Don't you trust us?" Lila demanded.

"It's not that," Jessica said warily. "It's just that I feel like I'm in the middle of some kind of dream or something. I just don't see why you'd be interested in someone like me."

Janet and Lila exchanged glances. "Maybe you

should tell her the other reason, Janet," Lila urged.

"What other reason?" Janet asked irritably.

"You know—" Lila gave her a meaningful look. "Tell her about how you have a crush on her brother."

"*Oh*," Janet said, a look of understanding dawning on her face. "*That* reason." She gave Jessica a sheepish grin. "OK, I admit it. I do sort of have a crush on your big brother."

Jessica almost seemed relieved. "I figured it was something like that!" she said.

"Well, can you blame me?" Janet said.

"A lot of girls do seem to like Steven," Jessica conceded. "They call him all the time." Her face darkened. "But he's been getting into a lot of trouble lately. Bad trouble."

Janet rubbed her hands together. "All the more reason to like him!" She gave Jessica an apologetic smile. "Sorry about that. I know I should have told you, but . . . well, even *I* get shy sometimes."

Ellen snorted. "Yeah, right."

Jessica hesitated. "Well, to tell you the truth, I'm kind of relieved. For a minute there I thought—" She rolled her eyes. "I actually thought maybe you were planning to play some kind of trick on me."

Janet and the others laughed. "A trick?" she

cried. "On Christmas Eve? Give me a break, Jess. Even the Sharks aren't that cruel!" She patted Jessica on the back. "So what do you say? Are you in?"

"I don't know. I guess—"

"She'll do it!" Lila exclaimed.

"First the makeover," Janet said. "Tamara, go get Lila's makeup kit. Kimberly, get some hair spray and mousse. *Lots* of it. Ellen, hand me your jacket."

"My jacket?" Ellen cried. "No way!"

"Yes way. Hand it over."

"What for?"

"For Jessica to wear tonight."

Ellen shook her head. "You think I'm going to let that—"

"Yes, I do," Janet said forcefully. "It's just for tonight, anyway. Later we'll get her one of her very own."

"I don't need Ellen's jacket," Jessica said quickly. "I brought my own."

"You want to look your best for your initiation, don't you?" Janet asked.

Jessica swallowed. "What initiation?"

"Oh, did I forget to mention that part?" Janet grinned. "You couldn't expect to become a Shark without some kind of initiation, could you?"

"I don't think I can do it tonight," Jessica said. "My mom—"

"Your mommy will understand," Janet said firmly. "Now, let's get down to business. First the makeover. Then the fun."

"Do you ever think about anything but food, Laura?" Elizabeth demanded, rushing into the Fowlers' huge, gleaming kitchen.

Laura pulled her head out of the refrigerator. "Now, *these* people know their junk food!" she exclaimed. She had an ice cream sandwich in one hand and a frozen burrito in the other.

"Hurry, Laura," Elizabeth said. "The Sharks just left with Jessica."

"I know. I know. Let me just—"

"Come *on*. I don't want to lose them!" Without waiting for Laura, Elizabeth ran through the marble foyer and straight through the closed door.

Jessica, the Sharks, and Jerry and Charlie were at the bottom of the long driveway. With Janet in the lead they headed down the street into the chill, damp night.

Just then Laura appeared beside Elizabeth. "Sorry to hold you up, Liz," she said, "but I do have this thing for ice cream sandwiches."

"Look what they did to Jessica," Elizabeth said

sadly. She pointed toward the street. "They put tons of makeup on her and teased her hair. She looks like a clown. Then they made her put on Ellen's jacket." She wrung her hands. "They said something about an initiation."

"I know," Laura said. "Charlie and Jerry were blabbing about it while I was trying to eat."

"Do you know what they're planning?"

Laura nodded. "I'm afraid so."

"Tell me." Elizabeth craned her neck to see Jessica. "No. You'd better tell me after we catch up to them. I don't want them to get out of my sight."

"Liz, I'm awfully full," Laura said. "I'm not up to any running. Or walking, for that matter."

"How much did you eat in there?"

"A gallon of rocky road and half a turkey. How about I just fly us to the spot where they're going? It'll save time and we'll be sure to get there before they do."

"Are you sure you can get us off the ground after eating that much? That's a lot of extra baggage."

"No, I'm not sure."

"Try anyway. This is important."

Laura rubbed her stomach. "OK. Try to picture City Hall. I need all the help I can get."

"City Hall?" Elizabeth cried. "We're trying to follow Jessica. Why City Hall?"

"You're arguing with one very nauseated angel, Liz," she warned. "Don't push your luck."

"Just hurry," Elizabeth urged. "I'm afraid they're going to do something horrible to Jessica."

Laura closed her eyes, and the wind picked up steam. "I'm afraid you may be right."

Twenty-two

❄

"Really nice landing, ace," Elizabeth complained, rubbing her rear end. "We're on the roof of a two-story building."

"Yeah, I know. City Hall." Laura clutched at her stomach. "Remind me to bring a barf bag next time I fly."

Elizabeth crawled carefully to the edge. The little town square was empty. The fountain in front of City Hall was turned off, but the Christmas lights on the big pine tree near the entrance were still lit. The streets were silent, the stores were dark. It was as if the whole town were holding its breath, waiting for Christmas to arrive.

Elizabeth stared straight down at the cement sidewalk beneath her. Her head started to spin and she jerked backward. "Couldn't you have landed us somewhere more convenient?" she asked. "Say, like the ground?"

"You think this is high? You ought to see where I've been hanging out for the last twenty-five years." Laura joined Elizabeth at the edge and sat down, dangling her legs over the side. "Besides, this is where they're bringing Jessica."

"Why?"

"See that star?" Laura pointed to the top of the peaked roof. At the very edge was a three-foot-high star made of wire and wrapped with white Christmas lights.

Elizabeth nodded. "They hang that star there every year."

"That's the initiation. They're going to dare her to climb up here and pull down the star."

"But she could never make it up here without a ladder," Elizabeth protested.

"Charlie said they were going to tell her to climb that big pine tree over there. The one right next to the building."

"The huge one with all the colored lights?"

"Yep. I suppose if she reaches just right, she might just be able to lean out from one of the branches and grab the edge of the building. She'd have to pull herself up and throw her legs onto the roof, though." Laura frowned.

"How's her upper-body strength?"

"Laura!" Elizabeth cried. "How can you joke about a thing like this? We're talking about my sister! She could really get hurt if she fell. She could even . . ." Her words faded away.

Laura patted her shoulder. "To tell you the truth, I have to make jokes. I can't really stand to think about it seriously."

Elizabeth scanned Main Street, a feeling of panic growing in her chest. There was no sign of Jessica and the Sharks yet. "How could Jessica be so stupid?" she shouted.

"Calm down, Liz. It's going to take them a while to get here. You might as well wait till you see what happens before you work yourself into a fit."

"It's Christmas Eve!" Elizabeth cried. "Why isn't she home safe and sound, where she belongs?"

"Sometimes people do stupid things, Liz. Even on Christmas Eve." Laura gave a short laugh. "Even yours truly."

There was a wistful sound in Laura's voice. Elizabeth looked over at her. "What are you talking about?" she asked.

"Well, let's see. There's that half a turkey, for starters."

"No. That's not what you meant," Elizabeth

said. "Did something happen to you on Christmas Eve? Something . . . a long time ago?"

"No biggie," Laura said shortly. "I was a stupid kid and I got what was coming to me." She dangled her legs back and forth. "We're not here to talk about me, Liz."

"Why not? We have to talk about something while we wait."

"Rule number seventy-eight in the trainee handbook. *Do not discuss PCs.*"

"PCs?"

"Previous Circumstances."

Elizabeth leaned back on her elbows against the rough shingles. "You're not exactly one to follow the rules, though."

Laura didn't answer. She stared at the big pine tree a few feet away. The wind whistled softly. The colored lights rattled as branches brushed the side of the building.

"Remember when you told me about how Patrick Morris ran away?" Elizabeth said.

Laura nodded. Her eyes welled with tears. She stared at the lights on the tree, her eyes mirroring their bright colors. "Another example of a stupid kid," she said. She gave a little shrug. "Takes one to know one."

"You ran away, too, didn't you?"

"Remind me to add *nosy* to your P-3 file."

Laura's voice had a tinge of anger. "You want the big sob story? Well, here are the highlights. My mom and dad got divorced, we didn't have much money, I got into a lot of trouble. We ended up at a shelter. Not as nice as the one Al and Suzannah are in, either. This one was a real dump."

"That must have been really hard for you."

"Yeah, well, it was a lot harder for my mom and my little sister, but of course I was too wrapped up in feeling sorry for myself to care." She let out a long sigh. "It got around to Christmastime and I decided to run away from the shelter. Real sweet, huh? Told you I have lousy people skills."

"How old were you?"

"Same age I am now. Same age I'll always be."

Laura fell silent. The breeze picked up and the trees began to talk, a low murmuring that sent a chill through Elizabeth. She gazed at the huge pine tree brushing the edge of the roof. *Please, Jessica,* she thought silently. *Please stay away. There's danger here.*

"So what happened?" she pressed, turning back to Laura. "You might as well tell me, Laura. You've gone this far."

Laura lay back on the roof, staring at the black sky. "I ended up in an abandoned house. Not exactly an improvement. And it was cold that night, even for L.A. Cold like it is tonight." She smiled. "There were a couple other kids there, too, high school age. A girl and a guy. And a pathetic stray cat. Pure black and skinny as a toothpick. We called him Cat."

Elizabeth laughed. "Very original."

"The guy had two cans of spaghetti he'd ripped off from a store that day. We built a little fire with a lighter and some newspaper and heated them up. I hadn't eaten all day, and man, I'm telling you, it was like eating at a gourmet restaurant. We three shared one can. We gave the other to Cat." She shook her head. "The whole can. He slept with me that night. He never stopped purring, not once."

"So you stayed there all night?"

"Well, yes and no. Yes, we stayed there. But we had a little heating problem we hadn't anticipated. Seems it's not a good idea to cook noodles in the middle of your living room. The whole place caught fire while we were sleeping."

Elizabeth gasped. "Is that how—" She couldn't bring herself to say the words out loud.

"We all managed to get out."

"Thank goodness." Elizabeth breathed a sigh of relief. "What a horrible way that would have been to . . ."

"It is, actually," Laura said in a faraway voice.

"But you said—"

"Oh, yeah. I got out. But that's when I proved how really stupid I am. I actually ran back into that inferno just to save that lousy cat." Laura laughed. "I don't even *like* cats. Anyway, that's life, as they say." She sighed. "I should have known. I mean, he was a black cat."

Elizabeth tried to find something to say, but her throat felt too tight to get any words out. She reached for Laura's icy fingers and held them. "Oh, Laura," she said, "I'm so sorry."

Laura sat up. "Me too. Not about what happened. I'm sorry that I was such a jerk, I didn't realize that running away from my problems wasn't the answer. Now, looking back, I can see that the bad times would have passed. I could have toughed it out. I mean, everybody has rough times. Everybody. Maybe, if there'd been someone around to help me through it, someone like you . . ." She looked at Elizabeth, her gray eyes serious. "You got your wish, Liz. Never to have been born. You want to know what mine is?"

Elizabeth nodded.

"I wish I'd stuck around. I wish I'd known that even when things seem really bad, there's no telling how it's all going to come out in the end.

It's like leaving in the middle of a movie. Who knows? It may just have a happy ending. There's no way to tell what effects you're having right now or what you might do in the future. Everything we do affects people, sometimes in ways we can't see." She bit her lower lip as tears streamed down her cheeks. "See, after I died, my little sister got really bummed out. She started hanging with the wrong kids. She even got into drugs."

"It wasn't your fault, Laura," Elizabeth said, feeling tears on her own cheeks.

"You don't understand. I didn't realize how much I meant to her. I didn't think my running away would matter—" Her voice cracked. "But it did matter. It mattered a lot. It's the Sweater Effect I told you about. Everything we do has consequences. Everybody matters." She looked away.

"Anyway, she took an overdose of drugs a few years later. And she died." Laura took a deep breath. "Now she's a vice president in charge of Angel Assignments." She laughed. "Figures she'd land a responsible job. She always *was* a better student. Me, I'm still trying to get it right." She looked at Elizabeth and shook her head. "And judging from the progress I'm making with you, I may *never* get it right."

Elizabeth didn't say anything. She didn't know what to say.

Laura stood and stretched her arms out over her head, breathing in the cold air. "Boy, I miss being alive. I miss roller coasters and the Beatles and sleeping in till noon with the covers over your head. Oh, yeah. And corn dogs. I really miss corn dogs." She looked down at Elizabeth and smiled. "So. Those are my PCs. Sorry you asked?"

"No," Elizabeth said softly. "I'm not sorry."

Laura put her hands on her hips. "And what have we learned from my tale of woe, class?" she asked in a schoolteacher voice. Elizabeth didn't answer.

"Come on, Liz," Laura chided. "You're the A student. We've been through a lot together. Hasn't any of this penetrated that thick skull of yours?"

"Laura!" Elizabeth pointed toward the street. A group of kids came into view under the glare of a streetlamp. "It's them!"

Lila and Janet led the way across the town square. Jessica trudged between them, glancing nervously from side to side. When they reached the fountain in front of City Hall, Janet held up her hand and the group came to a stop.

"It's time, Jessica," Janet announced. "You look like a Shark. Now let's see if you can *act* like one."

Twenty-three

❄

"Janet," Jessica said in a quavering voice, "I'm not so sure about this. I don't think I'm really cut out to be a Shark."

She took a step back, but the group closed around her like a tightening noose.

"Good girl, Jessica," Elizabeth whispered. She looked at Laura hopefully. "Maybe she won't go through with it."

"Maybe," Laura said darkly.

"You're not going to chicken out on us now, are you?" Janet demanded. "Not after all the time we've spent on you."

"You must have a hundred bucks' worth of my makeup on," Lila said, shaking her finger at Jessica. "And don't forget that's Ellen's jacket."

"You'd better not have stretched it, either," Ellen muttered.

Janet put her arm around Jessica's shoulders. "What we're trying to say is, we've *invested* in you, Jessica. You owe us. Besides, you don't even know what the initiation is yet. It's really very simple."

"A breeze," Ellen agreed.

Charlie spit onto the pavement. "Could we get on with this already?"

Jessica looked around at the group. "What would I have to do, exactly?"

"See that star up on top of the roof?" Janet asked, pointing. "All we want you to do is climb up there and pull down the star. Nothing to it."

"But how—" Jessica's eyes went wide. "You don't want me to climb that pine tree, do you?"

"No," Jerry said, "we want you to flap your little wings and fly up there."

Jessica looked confused. "Anyway, that star belongs to the city," she said. "It's a tradition, Janet. They put it up there every year. It would be wrong to take it."

"This isn't about right or wrong," Janet said firmly. "It's about becoming a Shark."

"An *associate* Shark," Ellen added.

"Besides," Lila said, "it's not like we're going to keep the star. We'll give it back. Right, Janet?"

"Oh, *right*." Janet nodded. "Sure thing."

Jessica walked over to the pine tree. She leaned her head back, staring up at the huge branches as they swayed in the wind.

"This is an easier initiation than the rest of us had to go through," Kimberly said in an encouraging voice. "We're making it simple because you're just starting out."

Jessica took a deep breath. "Well," she said. "I guess I could try."

"*No*, Jess," Elizabeth hissed. "Don't do it. It's too dangerous."

Jessica gazed back at the Sharks. "You promise you'll return the star tomorrow?"

"Right after we open our presents," Janet vowed. "Cross our hearts."

Jessica reached for one of the lower branches. She pulled on it, testing to see if it would hold her. Then she looked back at the Sharks with a determined smile. "OK," she said. "Here goes nothing."

"Wait!" Ellen cried, rushing forward. "Take off my jacket first!"

"Ellen!" Janet scolded.

"Well, what if she falls? That jacket cost a fortune."

"Here, Ellen." Jessica took off the jacket and handed it to her. Then she went back to the tree and pushed her way through the outside branches. "Wish me luck!" she called.

"You're going to need it!" Charlie muttered.

Elizabeth watched, her fists clenched by her sides, as Jessica climbed onto one of the lower branches. "Laura, can't you do something?" she demanded.

"I wish I could help her, Liz." Laura leaned over the side, watching as Jessica slowly made her way up. "But it's out of my hands."

Halfway up, Jessica paused to catch her breath. "How am I doing?" she called, half-hidden in the thick branches.

"Not bad," Janet said. "But could you step on it? It's cold out here."

"I think I broke a lightbulb with my foot," Jessica said.

Janet rolled her eyes. "We'll be sure to pay for it. Now, hurry up, would you?"

Jessica started to climb again. With each step, the branches shook and the tree swayed. The wind blew, steady and cold. Clouds shut out the moon. The Sharks stopped whispering and watched quietly. Except for the rustling branches and the sound of Jessica panting for air, the world was silent.

Elizabeth watched as Jessica neared the top of the tree. With every step, every branch, her heart lurched. It was like watching a horrible movie in slow motion. But there was no way she could stop the film. And no way she could leave the theater.

"Please stop, Jess," she whispered. If only there were some way she could reach Jessica, speak to her for just a moment. She thought of all the times she'd gotten Jessica out of tough jams. All the long talks, all the good advice, all the complicated plans to undo Jessica's mischief. Jessica counted on her. Jessica listened to her even when she didn't want to because she knew Elizabeth would always tell her the truth. They trusted each other and understood each other. And, most of all, they loved each other. But what good was all that now?

"I made it!" Jessica called to the Sharks when she was even with the roof. "Now what?"

"Now grab the roof, pull yourself up, and get the star," Janet instructed. But she sounded uncertain, as if she hadn't really expected Jessica to get that far.

Jessica looked at the roof, biting her lower lip. She stretched her right arm out as far as she could, but the edge of the roof was two feet from her grasp. She inched along the branch she was standing on and leaned out. The whole top of the tree leaned with her as if it were about to snap. She almost managed to touch the roof.

"It's too far," she yelled down to the Sharks. "I can't reach it."

"Don't stop now!" Charlie called. "You're almost there."

"I don't know, Charlie," Tamara said. "I don't think she can make it."

"Try swaying back and forth," Lila suggested. "You know—to get some momentum."

Ellen shook her head grimly. "I'm glad she took my jacket off."

Elizabeth felt panic rising in her throat. She grabbed Laura, glaring into her eyes. "I don't want to see this, Laura," she cried. "Don't make me."

"This is what you wanted, Liz," Laura said. "This is what you wished for."

Across town square, on Main Street, a pair of headlights appeared. "Someone's coming," Charlie hissed. "Should we leave?"

"And miss the best part?" Jerry said. "Come on, Jessica, go for it!"

Jessica took a deep breath. With one hand anchored on the trunk, she leaned far out over the square like a child standing on a swing. The whole tree moved with her, bending and groaning as if it were caught in a hurricane. With all her might Jessica leaned the other direction. Slowly the tree swayed back toward the building.

Needles slapped against the brick. A branch cracked. Jessica reached out her right hand and her fingers brushed the edge of the roof. She grabbed hold with all her might. Her left hand released the trunk and the tree pulled away, leaving her hanging, suspended over the sidewalk below by one hand.

"Help!" she screamed, frantically clawing at the roof with her free hand. "Help me!"

A bright light from a slow-moving car flashed across the horrified faces of the Sharks. "What's going on here?" came a woman's voice.

"Cops!" Charlie screamed. "Run for it!"

The Sharks scattered, lost in the darkness and the cover of trees.

Jessica's fingernails scraped along the shingles.

"Please!" Elizabeth screamed with all her might. "Please, Laura! Don't let it happen! This isn't what I wished for. This isn't what I want!" She sobbed helplessly. "Please, please, let me go back. I'll do anything to get back!"

The policewoman turned her flashlight on the front of City Hall.

"Please," Jessica whispered in a strangled voice. "Someone help me."

"Please let me go back," Elizabeth sobbed again.

The beam danced over the red brick building just in time to catch the look of pure terror on Jessica's face as her fingers slipped the last few inches.

Twenty-four

❄

The world began to spin and flicker. Laura reached for Elizabeth's hand. "You know, Liz?" she whispered. "I may just have gotten it right after all."

Elizabeth tried to speak, but her words seemed to evaporate in the shimmering air. She was in the middle of a giant carousel. The buildings and trees reeled around her faster and faster until they blurred into a whirlpool of color, but she and Laura remained perfectly still.

"Do me a favor, will you?" Laura asked. Her eyes filled with tears. "Buy yourself a corn dog when you get back, OK?"

She smiled. It was a sweet, sad smile, part longing and part hope. Then she let go of Elizabeth's hand and vanished into the mist.

Elizabeth closed her eyes and held her breath and waited.

The sky had changed. That was the first thing Elizabeth noticed when she opened her eyes. The moon was full. The clouds were gone. And the sky was crowded with stars, white and palest gold and icy blue, like a field of wildflowers. Elizabeth heard laughter and spun around. She was outside the middle-school auditorium. Light poured through the windows. She could see red and green balloons. Students and parents and little children filled the huge room. A carol was playing over the loudspeaker. She listened for a moment. "The Little Drummer Boy."

Cautiously Elizabeth crept over to one of the windows. Could it be that she was really back? Back in her old Sweet Valley? *Please let me be home,* she pleaded silently. She looked over her shoulder. "Laura?" she whispered. "Are you there?"

The leaves in a nearby oak tree rustled softly. Elizabeth waited. There was no sign of Laura.

"Elizabeth? Is that you?"

Someone could see her! Someone was talking to her!

Elizabeth turned. There in the doorway were Sophia and Sarah. Sophia, smiling radiantly. And Sarah, alive and well.

With tears flowing down her cheeks, Elizabeth ran over and hugged them both. "I have never in my entire life been so happy to see two people!" she cried. She grinned at Sarah. "You're OK. You're really OK."

"Of course I'm OK," Sarah said, laughing. She grabbed Elizabeth's arm. "Are *you* OK?"

"I'm better than OK. I'm great. I'm incredible," Elizabeth said. She couldn't help giggling. "Merry Christmas."

"Merry Christmas," Sarah said. She pulled on Elizabeth's arm. "Come on. I know some people who are going to be pretty happy to see you, too."

They led Elizabeth inside. She looked around the room in amazement. This was nothing like the party Laura had shown her. The room was laden with balloons and streamers and crepe paper hanging from the ceiling. A table in the corner was weighed down with cookies and punch and a beautiful white cake with red and green icing.

She gazed at the faces in the room. The auditorium was packed with people. But somehow it seemed as though the party hadn't started yet. People weren't eating or talking or dancing. They seemed to be waiting.

Practically everyone she knew was here. Brooke and Mary. Patrick and Denny. Todd and

Ken and Amy and Maria. Steven and Tony Rizzo. Winston and Ken. And the Unicorns, all of them dressed, as she knew they would be, in purple.

"I'm home," Elizabeth whispered.

"Hey, everybody!" Sophia called. "Look who's here!"

Everyone turned to stare. The whole room fell silent. All eyes were on Elizabeth.

Suddenly the crowd parted and Elizabeth heard rushing footsteps.

"Elizabeth!" Jessica cried, flying toward her. She wrapped her arms around Elizabeth and spun her in a circle as the crowd erupted in applause.

"Oh, Lizzie," Jessica said, half sobbing, half laughing. "We were so worried about you! Where have you been?"

"Well—" Elizabeth hesitated. "I went to the mall. . . ."

"We all felt so awful and stupid when we heard," Jessica said in a rush.

"Heard?" Elizabeth echoed.

Suzannah appeared on the edge of the crowd, smiling shyly. "I called your house this afternoon, Elizabeth," she explained. "I wanted to tell you that my dad made it home safe and sound. He'd been snowed in. I asked Jessica to tell you that you could have your money back—"

"And *that's* when we put two and two together and realized what had really happened," Jessica finished.

Mrs. Glass pushed her way through the crowd. A tall man with a red beard was with her. He was holding Al in his arms.

"Thank goodness you're all right," Mrs. Glass said, giving Elizabeth a long, hard hug.

"This is Lisbeth, Daddy," Al announced. "She's our bestest friend!"

Mr. Glass extended his hand. "It's good to meet you, Elizabeth," he said. "I can't thank you enough for all you did to help my family."

"We got a new 'partment, Lisabeth!" Al exclaimed. "Your daddy helped us find it!"

Elizabeth looked over at Jessica in confusion. "Dad?"

Jessica nodded. "When we figured out what had happened, we told Mom and Dad. Turns out Dad knew someone with a three-bedroom apartment for rent."

"And it has even *bigger* swings!" Al exclaimed.

Just then Elizabeth caught sight of two familiar faces in the crowd. "Mom!" she cried. "Dad!" She ran to hug them close. "Sweetheart," Mrs. Wakefield said, "you did a wonderful thing. If only we'd known what was going on, we could have helped you sooner."

Elizabeth looked at her mother, then at her father, then back again. They looked so young, so happy and full of love. She glanced at her father's hand and grinned. His gold wedding band caught the light and sparkled.

"What are you looking at, honey?" he asked.

"Oh, nothing," Elizabeth said. "I'm just glad to see that nothing changed while I was gone."

Amy slapped her on the back. "Thank goodness you're finally here!" she exclaimed. "We were so worried."

Todd came over and put his arm around her shoulders. "Hey, Elizabeth. Merry Christmas."

Elizabeth looked at Todd. "You're not mad?"

"Mad?" Todd laughed. "Only that you took so long to get to this party. I mean, you *are* the guest of honor."

"What are you talking about?" Elizabeth asked.

Jessica smiled at Elizabeth. "I *did* decide on a theme after all. I got my idea from you. See that barrel over there? It's for donations to the homeless shelter."

"My dad put in a check for a thousand bucks," Lila said proudly.

"And I put in a nickel!" Al added.

Jessica put her arm around Elizabeth's shoulders. "But you haven't seen the best part yet," she said. She pointed toward the far wall, where a huge banner was hanging.

Elizabeth stared in disbelief at the bright red letters. MERRY CHRISTMAS, ELIZABETH! SWEET VALLEY LOVES YOU!

The words blurred as tears spilled down her cheeks. She gazed at the smiling faces of her family and her friends. "I love you, too," she whispered.

Jessica took Elizabeth's hand, led her through the crowd to the refreshments table, and poured two cups of punch. She handed one to Elizabeth, then held up her hand. "I want to make a toast!" Jessica announced.

After a few moments the crowd quieted.

"I'd like to make a toast to Elizabeth Wakefield," Jessica said, "the very best sister in the entire world!"

The crowd cheered, but Elizabeth wasn't listening. She was staring intently at the bottom tier of the cake. Someone had decided to take an early taste and had left behind a nice, neat, finger-sized hole.

Laura. "I understand now, Laura," Elizabeth whispered. "You did get it right after all."

"What did you say, Lizzie?" Jessica asked, leaning close.

Elizabeth smiled. "I was just wondering," she said. "Do you know anywhere I could get a corn dog on Christmas Eve?"

SIGN UP FOR THE SWEET VALLEY HIGH® FAN CLUB!

Hey, girls! Get all the gossip on Sweet Valley High's® most popular teenagers when you join our fantastic Fan Club! As a member, you'll get all of this really cool stuff:

- Membership Card with your own personal Fan Club ID number
- A Sweet Valley High® Secret Treasure Box
- Sweet Valley High® Stationery
- Official Fan Club Pencil (for secret note writing!)
- Three Bookmarks
- A "Members Only" Door Hanger
- Two Skeins of J. & P. Coats® Embroidery Floss with flower barrette instruction leaflet
- Two editions of *The Oracle* newsletter
- Plus exclusive Sweet Valley High® product offers, special savings, contests, and much more!

Be the first to find out what Jessica & Elizabeth Wakefield are up to by joining the Sweet Valley High® Fan Club for the one-year membership fee of only $6.95 each for U.S. residents, $8.25 for Canadian residents (U.S. currency). Includes shipping & handling.

Send a check or money order (do not send cash) made payable to "Sweet Valley High® Fan Club" along with this form to:

SWEET VALLEY HIGH® FAN CLUB, BOX 3919-B, SCHAUMBURG, IL 60168-3919

NAME_____
(Please print clearly)

ADDRESS_____

CITY_____ STATE _____ ZIP_____
(Required)

AGE_____ BIRTHDAY_____ /_____ /_____

Offer good while supplies last. Allow 6-8 weeks after check clearance for delivery. Addresses without ZIP codes cannot be honored. Offer good in USA & Canada only. Void where prohibited by law.
©1993 by Francine Pascal   LCI-1383-193

☎
1 (800) I LUV BKS!

If you'd like to hear more about your
favorite young adult novels and writers . . .
OR
If you'd like to tell us what you thought
of this book or other books
you've recently read . . .

CALL US at 1(800) I LUV BKS
[1(800) 458-8257]
Monday to Friday, 9AM – 8PM EST

You'll hear a new message about books and
other interesting subjects each month.

**The call is free, but please get
your parents' permission first.**